Angry Young Women in Low-Rise Jeans with High-Class Issues

by

Matt Morillo

SAMUEL FRENCH

FOUNDED 1830

NEW YORK HOLLYWOOD LONDON TORONTO

SAMUELFRENCH.COM

Cover photo by Rich Barbadillo and cover design by Sara Steigerwald

Cover Photo consists of original New York cast members: Front Row L to R: Devon Pipars, Jessica Durdock, Rachel Nau, Martin Friedrichs. Back Row L to R: Angelique Letizia, Nick Coleman, Jessica Durdock, Tom Pilutik.

ISBN 978-0-573-66024-5   Printed in U.S.A.   #3171

IMPORTANT BILLING AND CREDIT
REQUIREMENTS

ANGRY YOUNG WOMEN IN LOW-RISE JEANS WITH HIGH-CLASS ISSUES
is a collection of five short comedies about young women and the various issues they confront today.

Throughout the five pieces, the women of New York go head to head with such issues as bikini waxes, low-rise jeans, thongs, sexual fantasies, public displays of affection, birth control drugs, their side effects, mean teenage kids on the subway, Electra complexes, traumatic memories of the first sexual experience, traumatic memories of last night's sexual experience, sympathy sex, the double standard of nudity in movies, the artistic integrity of vaginas and penises in independent film, and of course...men.

The first piece, *My Last Thong*, is a comedic monologue in which Soleil, tired of the constantly diminishing size of women's fashions, puts her foot down and swears to never wear another thong.

The second show is a one-act play, *Playtime in the Park*. In this piece Rebecca and Sarah struggle with the burden of being the subject of some really raunchy and offensive sexual fantasies.

In *Unprotected Sex*, also a one-act play, Rachel finds her birth control pill-induced mood swings too much to handle and takes out her frustrations on her boyfriend and his best friend while they try to watch a hockey game.

Next is another comedic monologue, *The Miseducation of Elissa*. Elissa, fed up with her bad luck with men, blames her loving, supportive and generous father for her problems. In her opinion, if he wasn't so nice to her, she would never had developed a trust for men and therefore would not be in the situation she is in right now.

The finale is another one-act play, *The Nude Scene*. In this play, Jennifer has second thoughts about her first career topless scene. She enlists the help of Katy, her childhood friend, to help her get through this ordeal.

By using minimal sets and a cast that can play multiple roles, these shows can be produced on a very small budget. In its entirety, without an intermission, the show should run about eighty-five minutes. At this length, the show will provide an enjoyable and funny experience for the audience.

EXTRA SPECIAL ACKNOWLEDGEMENT

CRYSTAL FIELD

AND

THEATER FOR THE NEW CITY

No one has been more integral to the success of this play than Crystal Field and all the fine people at the Theater for the New City. After seeing us in our initial run in the winter of 2006, they selected this show for a featured spot in their Lower East Side Festival of the Arts. Then they presented us for a six-week run, which earned a two-week extension, in the winter of 2007. It was this run which truly put this show on the map, leading to an off-Broadway run and two runs in Sydney, Australia.

We cannot thank them enough for their support and for granting us the opportunity to showcase this play.

Organizations like Theater for the New City are very difficult to find these days, organizations that nurture emerging artists and allow them to grow. Through the years, their commitment to new playwrights and new works has helped launch the careers of many great, well-known playwrights, actors and artists of all kinds. Here's to hoping that we will one day be added to that list!

Once again, a great many thanks to Crystal Field and Theater for the New City. Please support this organization. They are doing some amazing things.

www.theaterforthenewcity.net

SPECIAL THANKS

Richard West, Sara Steigerwald, Mike Farrell, SuperGrip, Kenny Yee,
The Gorney Family, The Duo Theater, Michaelangelo Alasa', Tony Ruiz,
The Hicksville Crew, Kara Lewis, Lotus, Adrian Gallard, Mark Marcante,
Angelina Soriano, Michael Sgouros, The Players Theater, Don Lewis,
Chris Botta, The New York Islanders, Maria Micheles, The Barbarians,
PIP Printing of Hicksville, Dan Kelley, Jerry Jaffe, Jonathan Weber,
Candice Burridge, Lisa Sgouros, Carlo Rivieccio, Christy Benanti, Kristin
Smith, Chris Force, Jon D. Andreadakis, Richard Reta, Teri Lea Yoest,
Malek Hanna, Kevin Mazeski and of course, all of our friends and family
for their support!

ANGRY YOUNG WOMEN IN LOW-RISE JEANS WITH HIGH-CLASS ISSUES
was first produced from January 19th through February 25th of 2006 at
the Duo Theater at 62 East 4th Street in New York City.

Original Cast was:

SOLEIL . . . . Jessica Durdock
RONNIE . . . . Nick Coleman
REBECCA . . . . Angelique Letizia
SARAH . . . . Devon Pipars
BRIAN . . . . Major Dodge
JOE . . . . Tom Pilutik
RACHEL . . . . Jessica Durdock
ELISSA . . . . Rachel Nau
JENNIFER . . . . Devon Pipars
KATY . . . . Jessica Durdock
SPENCER . . . . Tom Pilutik
KRISTOFF . . . . Jason Drumwright
BARRY . . . . Major Dodge

Producers . . . . Jessica Durdock, Matt Morillo and Richard Barbadillo, Jr.
Set Design . . . . Aaron Glazer
Lighting Design . . . . Amith A. Chandrashaker
Publicity . . . . Jonathan Slaff and Associates
Marketing Service . . . . Barbara Okishoff and Artvoice

After being selected for the Lower East Side Festival of the Arts on May
28th, 2006 at the legendary Theater for the New City at 155 1st Ave
in New York City, *ANGRY YOUNG WOMEN IN LOW-RISE JEANS WITH
HIGH-CLASS ISSUES* was then presented by Crystal Field and the Theater for the New City from January 4th through February 24th, 2007.

ANGRY YOUNG WOMEN IN LOW-RISE JEANS WITH HIGH-CLASS ISSUES was first produced off-Broadway from July 12, through October 20, 2007 at The Players Theatre at 115 MacDougal Street in New York City. The original Cast was as follows:

SOLEIL . . . . Devon Pipars
RONNIE . . . . Martin Friedrichs
REBECCA . . . . Angelique Letizia
SARAH . . . . Jessica Durdock
BRIAN . . . . Nick Coleman
JOE . . . . Tom Pilutik
RACHEL . . . . Rachel Nau
ELISSA . . . . Angelique Letizia
JENNIFER . . . . Rachel Nau
KATY . . . . Jessica Durdock
SPENCER . . . . Tom Pilutik
KRISTOFF . . . . Nick Coleman
BARRY . . . . Martin Friedrichs
HOSTESS . . . . Brooke Hasalton

Producers . . . . Jessica Durdock, Matt Morillo and Richard Barbadillo, Jr.
Set Design . . . . Jana Mattioli
Lighting Design . . . . Amith A. Chandrashaker
Publicity . . . . Jonathan Slaff and Associates

NOTES FOR PRODUCERS

All licensees are required to use the **ANGRY YOUNG WOMEN IN LOW-RISE JEANS WITH HIGH-CLASS ISSUES** logo and slogan, "Even Though It's A Play, It Doesn't Suck", including the "TM" notation, in their marketing materials.

Producers are free to use any kind of photo/graphic they wish, but they must use the logo and slogan with it. It is not required that producers use the logo in color, as budget restraints may not allow it. Contact Samuel French Inc. for the materials.

In the program, the following must be credited:

"The Angry Young Women In Low-Rise Jeans With High-Class Issues title and slogan, "Even Though It's A Play, It Doesn't Suck" is the exclusive property of KADM Productions, LLC. Trademark is pending. The design was originally created by Sara Steigerwald of www.exquisitebeast.com."

"For Angry Young Women In Low-Rise Jeans With High-Class Issues merchandise and licensing opportunities, visit www.angryyoungwomen.net"

Credit for the playwright must be as follows:
Matt Morillo (Writer) Filmmaker/Playwright Matt Morillo has also written the play, All Aboard the Marriage Hearse, which is also published by Samuel French, Inc. For more information on his films, visit www.kadm.com. To visit his blog, go to www.thecynicaloptimist.net.

Producers should feel free to cast different body types for Sarah, Rachel, Jennifer and Katy. Although specific references are made in the script to Rachel, Jennifer and Katy having large chests and Sarah having a small chest, producers should just alter the few lines of dialogue that make specific references to their respective chests in event that their selected actor does not exactly fit the type.

In the event of budget constraints, producers should not feel obligated to erect a brick wall, just use the integral pieces of the set.

MY LAST THONG

Cast of Characters

SOLEIL: Brunette, late 20's. She's the type who can capti-
vate a room with either her looks or her intelligence.
She's all business and won't hesitate to tell you.

Scene

A conference room somewhere in New York City.

Time

Right now.

ACT I

Scene 1

(*One light rises illuminating a small area in the middle of the stage. The rest of the stage remains dark.*

SOLEIL, *wearing a no-nonsense black pantsuit, walks out onto the stage with a pair of scissors in one hand and a piece of paper in the other.*

She stops in the center of the stage.)

SOLEIL. For several years now, I've had a dream. A beautiful dream. A dream that one day it would once again be socially acceptable for a woman to wear a pair of underwear that doesn't stick up her behind. A dream that one day a woman could once again have some hair on her private parts. A dream that one day a woman could once again wear a pair of jeans that doesn't show off her butt crack and thong. Basically, a dream that one day women wouldn't have to go to these ridiculous extremes to be considered sexy. Well my friends, it appears that a part of this dream just might have come true. Check this out.

I just cut this out of a magazine. This article says, and I quote, "The end of the low-rise jeans craze is upon us as stores stock up on new styles of higher-waisted pants. The gap between the belly button and the hip bone is shrinking once again." And blah, blah, blah.

Aren't you thrilled to hear this? I can't be the only one who was getting a little tired of seeing plumber's crack and g-strings everywhere, was I? You have to admit it was getting out of hand.

I mean, just a few weeks ago, I was meeting my girlfriends for happy hour. So I get to the bar and right

12

before I walk in, what do I see? My four friends sitting down on this bench with their backs against the floor to ceiling front window. Well, I actually didn't see them, what I saw was their butt cracks. One after the other, after the other I saw Chrissy's then Ashley's then Debbie's then Maggie's.

Four girl butts staring out onto Park Avenue for all of New York to see. I swear to God, I had half a mind to walk in their and drop change down their pants, bing, bing, bing, bing, you know, just to teach them a lesson.

But I guess I can't be a hypocrite about it because after a few cocktails I sat down right next to them on that bench and showed all the world my coin slot too.

And I have to say it is a little disconcerting that for the first twenty three years of my life, the only people who saw my ass were my mommy and daddy when they changed my diaper and the select few boys that I hopped into bed with. But I'm sad to say that in recent years, that number has skyrocketed thanks to these infernal low-rise jeans.

But maybe we ladies shouldn't complain. Maybe we should just be happy that it may be over. I'm serious. Because I actually thought waistlines would continue to drop. I did. I had this vision of Paris Hilton on the cover of Maxim posing in her super-super-low-rise jeans showing off a little bit of clit cleavage.

Yes, that's right. Clit cleavage. I said it. And you were worried we were headed there too, weren't you? Or maybe you were thinking that pubic hair would come back into style and it would be fashionable to have some happy trail poking up from our low-risers. Sexy, huh?

And while I'm on the subject, let's talk about those pesky pubes, shall we? Here's my question, if jeans are really on the rise, does this mean we can calm down with the trimming and tweezing? I'm not suggesting we go back to the 1970's Sherwood Forest look, but maybe we can find a happy medium because this situation is out of control too, isn't it? I mean, there was a reason they called it bush. What's wrong with bringing a little of that back?

Christ, I remember when I was eighteen and shaving wasn't "in" yet. My boyfriend at the time asked me to shave it and I told him no because the idea of sticking a razor down there or waxing it seemed sadistic. But now, not only do I shave it, I periodically pay a complete stranger to tear my pubes out with hot wax and gauze strips while I lay spread eagle on a table with Enya playing in the background. What the fuck?

You know when I knew we were nearing the apocalypse? When my mother started shaving her vagina. Oh yeah. I'm not joking. My mother is a fifty-five year old grandmother and she grooms herself into one of those disgusting landing strip things. Oh my God it's so gross. In fact, the other day she offered to treat me to a Brazilian bikini wax.

Not only does that mean she was thinking about my vagina, she was thinking about styling it. Nice mother-daughter bonding activity, huh? Fathers and sons go to the ball game together while mothers and daughters get their twats trimmed together.

How nice.

And here's the kicker on that one. Back in the 60's, my mom was a feminist who burned her bras. I actually remember when I was a little girl and she didn't even shave her armpits. Isn't that something? I mean when did this happen? I thought the whole idea of feminism is to be known for your mind instead of your hoo ha.

I'm serious. When did being a strong independent woman cease to be a cool thing to do? And why do we continue to conform? Is it for men? Christ, I hope not because let's be honest, no guy is going to turn down sex just because your jeans come up to your waist or because you have a big old muff or because your underwear covers your whole ass. Am I right?

And speaking of which, isn't it time we went back to
normal-sized underwear? Because this shit is out of
hand too. I really thought thongs would be a 90's thing
but there's no end in sight, is there? For Christ's sake,
do you realize that they are making maternity thongs
now? Now I've never been pregnant, but I'm guess-
ing it's uncomfortable enough without these things
crammed up your ass. And not for nothing, when your
stomach is out to here and you're having morning sick-
ness and bizarre cravings and your boobs are swollen...
I think panty lines are the least of your problems. Am
I wrong? And while I'm still on the subject of thongs,
let me ask a question; why is women's underwear getting smaller and men's underwear getting bigger?
Think about it. Guys used to wear briefs and we used
to wear full backs. Now guys wear boxers and we wear
thongs. What's next? Are guys going to start wearing
sweatpants for underwear while we wear little adhesive
patches down here?

Okay, well maybe the adhesive patch thing is a little
extreme, we'll probably never get there. Because if we
did, they wouldn't have anywhere to put those ridiculous little decorations that they now put on the ass
crack area of our thongs. You know what I'm talking
about? Whose idea was this? Mmmm, let's put a little
heart or a bow or a diamond or a rhinestone or little
fucking annoying butterfly right here. Yeah. A butterfly
right here!

(*pointing to ass crack area*)

Ladies, they have us wearing jewelry on our ass cracks.
They are telling us that we are expected to show this
shit off and Goddamnit, I've had enough.

Look, facts are fact, women are always going to have
more grooming to do than men. They're always going
to be expected to show more skin. That's just the way
it is. I'm always going to have to shave my legs, my boyfriend never will. When I go to the beach, men literally
see me in my bra and panties, or at least the kind of

panties I would've worn ten years ago.

But I digress. My point is that the revolution begins now and since the low-rise jeans trend appears to be cooling off, I'm going to jump right in. I'm going to go to the store right now and buy some real jeans. I'll buy men's jeans if I have to. In fact, I might just go to a thrift store and find some of those Jordache jeans women wore in the 80's. You know the ones I'm talking about? They come up to here

(pointing at her chest)

and if you want something out of your back pocket you have to go like this.

(Reaches over her shoulder)

Now, for step two of the revolution, I am going to stop shaving and waxing my genitalia. Never again will I let another stranger tear out my pubes. And, guys, don't worry, I'm not going to go crazy, but I'm going to grow a little something, something down there. And, you know what, I don't care what my boyfriend says. In fact, if he even dares to complain I can promise you that these lips will be sealed

(pointing to crotch)

and I will just run these lips non-stop.

(pointing to her mouth)

How do you like that? And finally, for step three, no more thongs. And I don't care what they decorate them with. I don't care if they use pearls, rubies, gold, silver, or every coin from the goddamn Franklin Mint. It doesn't matter. I will never cram anything up this ass again. And I don't care what my boyfriend says about that either because, now that I think about it I've never liked these fucking things anyway. I've just allowed myself to get used to them but they are really fucking irritating so I am getting the fuck out of here now and I'm going to make shopping for new underwear my number one priority because I can't take this anymore.

(**SOLEIL** *starts to leave, but she stops. She looks down at the scissors.*)

Oh I almost forgot.

(*She pulls the thong strap out of one side, she cuts it with the scissor. She pulls the other strap out, cuts it. She reaches into her pants and pulls on the underwear. She struggles.*

Now she's got it. She yanks that thong out of her pants and hold it over her hear like captured prey.)

The revolution has begun!

(*She throws the thong down and proudly marches off stage. The lights go down.*)

PLAYTIME IN THE PARK

Cast of Characters

REBECCA: Dark hair, early thirties, loud and boisterous. She's a sorority girl who never matured.

RONNIE: Dark hair, late twenties. A beer guzzling, fun loving guy.

SARAH: Blonde, eighteen. An idealistic, hip, but angry young girl. Cute as a button.

Scene

A bench in Central Park.

Time

This afternoon.

ACT I

Scene I

(*The lights come up to reveal a bench, a trash can and a brick wall with a restroom sign on the wall stage left that says, "MEN" and a restroom sign on the wall stage right that says, "WOMEN."*)

REBECCA *and* **RONNIE** *make out on the bench. They are really going at it as if no one can see. They're not even coming up for air.* **RONNIE** *puts his hand on her breast.*

She lays down on the bench and pulls him on top of her. It's hot and heavy. They don't care who sees.

SARAH, *backpack in hand, enters the stage and approaches the bench. She slows down and looks over at the couple. They don't notice her.*

REBECCA, *still not noticing* **SARAH**, *climbs on top of* **RONNIE**. *Her thong creeps up from her pants.*

SARAH *realizes who they are and rolls her eyes.*

SARAH *slams her backpack to the ground.*

They still don't notice her. They're too into their make out session.

SARAH *grabs the strap of* **REBECCA**'s *thong and SNAPS it.*

REBECCA *YELPS.*)

SARAH. Get a room!

That snaps them out of it.

REBECCA. (*jumps off the bench and puts her arm around* **SARAH**) Oh good. Sarah.

SARAH. You do realize that you're in Central Park, it's the middle of the day and there are families and children around?

RONNIE. You said she was a smart one.

REBECCA. I said she was smart and cute. I can't believe this is my little cousin. I used to babysit her, bathe her, I used to change her diapers and –

SARAH. He gets the point.

RONNIE. She's hot. All the women in your family are hot. You both are hot, your mother's hot, your aunts, your cousins. There's some good genes in your family.

SARAH. (*Turns to* **RONNIE**.) I don't mean to be rude but who the hell are you?

RONNIE. I'm sorry. I've heard so much about you I feel like I know you already. I'm Ronnie.

(*He puts his hand out for* **SARAH** *to shake it. She doesn't.* **REBECCA** *grabs her hand and puts it out so* **RONNIE** *can shake it.*)

REBECCA. He's joining us for lunch.

SARAH. But I told you I have something to talk to you about.

REBECCA. I know and Ronnie's an expert on these matters. He's a guy.

RONNIE. I am most definitely that.

SARAH. But this is private.

RONNIE. Don't worry I've heard it all before.

REBECCA. Yes. He's heard it all before and done it all before and we're taking you to lunch to celebrate.

RONNIE. Oh yes, by the way, congratulations.

SARAH. Congratulations for what?

RONNIE. For...the thing we're celebrating...you know.

SARAH. You know what?

REBECCA. What's wrong with you? Ronnie's congratulating you on losing your virginity.

(**REBECCA** *playfully slaps* **SARAH** *in the crotch.*)

SARAH. You told him?

REBECCA. It kind of slipped out.

SARAH. Things like this don't just slip out, Rebecca.

RONNIE. It's no big deal. We've all been through it.

SARAH. This is so embarrassing.

RONNIE. Come on. It can't be more embarrassing than my first time. When I lost my virginity, I busted the second I stuck it in.

SARAH. Oh my God!

REBECCA. Ronnie, that's a beautiful story but not now.

RONNIE. Okay. Sorry.

(**RONNIE** *retreats back to the bench.* **REBECCA** *approaches* **SARAH**.)

REBECCA. Just ignore that last comment.

SARAH. I want to talk to you and only you. This is serious and I –

RONNIE. Oh my God. She didn't go through with it.

SARAH. Mind your business.

(**RONNIE** *gets up and looks in her eyes.* **SARAH** *backs away.*)

RONNIE. I can see it. She didn't. Look in her eyes.

REBECCA. Is that true? You didn't go through with it?

SARAH. That's what I have to talk to you about.

RONNIE. I told you. She's not acting like someone who just got laid.

SARAH. Rebecca! Leash your dog now!

REBECCA. Ronnie, sit.

(*He does.*)

SARAH. I want him out of here right now.

REBECCA. Would you please stop acting like a child?

SARAH. Hello! You're thirty years old and you're sucking face in the park like a teenager!

REBECCA. I am not thirty!

(*The girls start screaming uncontrollably at each other.*
RONNIE *gets up and tries to step between them.*)

RONNIE. Girls –

SARAH. That's right. You're not thirty. I remember your thirtieth birthday party three years ago –

REBECCA. What is wrong with you? Don't you know not to say –

SARAH. Don't you tell me! You are the rudest person –

(**RONNIE** *butts his head in between them.*)

RONNIE. Girls, girls, girls. I can go. It's no big deal.

SARAH. Thank you!   **REBECCA.** No!

REBECCA. I want you to have lunch with us and I want Sarah to get your perspective on this.

SARAH. I don't give a shit what this clown has to say.

REBECCA. Don't call him a clown.

SARAH. What would you call him?

RONNIE. Alright, alright. I'll tell you what. I can smell those hot dogs from here. Why don't I go get us some?

REBECCA. Yes. I like mine plain please.

RONNIE. What about you, Sarah?

SARAH. You mean she told you I'm a virgin but not a vegetarian.

RONNIE. Vegetarian?

REBECCA. Yes, like a virgin. She doesn't eat meat. Just get her a pretzel or a knish.

RONNIE. I'm on it. I'll be back in a minute.

SARAH. Oh a minute, is that all it takes?

RONNIE. You're cute, Sarah.

REBECCA. She's rude. Just hurry back.

RONNIE. Will do.

(**RONNIE** *runs off stage.*)

REBECCA. What is the matter with you? That was completely unacceptable!

SARAH. You're goddamn right it was. How dare you tell a

complete stranger my private business.

REBECCA. Okay, okay, I'm sorry. I didn't realize your virginity was going to be a national crisis. I thought we were just going to talk about sex and have some fun and Ronnie's fun and he likes to talk about sex so I didn't think it would be a big deal.

SARAH. I can't believe you.

REBECCA. I said I was sorry.

SARAH. Well you should know better.

REBECCA. And you should know better too.

SARAH. Me?

REBECCA. Yes, you. If you met the guy of your dreams and you brought him out to meet me I wouldn't treat him like that, no matter what.

SARAH. That's the guy of your dreams?

REBECCA. I think so.

SARAH. You don't ask for much.

REBECCA. Oh please. He is the most fun guy I've ever met. We met Friday night and we have not been apart since and I think he's the one even though he's not even Jewish. But I don't care about that anymore. He said he'll get married in a temple.

SARAH. I guess what they say is true. Your standards get lower as you get older.

REBECCA. No. They just mature. You start looking for a real guy. Not just looks and money. Other things matter.

SARAH. Oh yeah. Like what?

REBECCA. For example, do you know how many orgasms I had last night?

SARAH. I don't want to know.

REBECCA. Fine. Fun fact. He's circumcised even though he's not Jewish.

SARAH. Don't be so stupid. Most guys are today.

REBECCA. True but on the off chance you get one that's not, all that extra skin, yuck. It looks like a pig in a blanket.

SARAH. Can we stop talking about extra skin and orgasms and talk about me please?

REBECCA. Okay, okay. So is this true? Did you chicken out?

SARAH. Please don't put it that way.

REBECCA. Are you still a virgin?

SARAH. Technically.

REBECCA. Technically?

SARAH. Well –

REBECCA. Did he stick his penis in you?!

SARAH. No, he didn't and yes, I'm still a virgin.

REBECCA. Okay, so what happened?

SARAH. Okay. So remember, Anthony and I had this beautiful night planned. He was having me over and he was going to cook me a candlelight dinner and it was going to be really special and I was going to...you know.

REBECCA. Yes of course.

SARAH. Well. He said something I think I didn't like. Something about me. Something possibly perverted about me.

REBECCA. And?

SARAH. And it freaked me out so I told him that I got called into work and I broke our date.

REBECCA. What did he say?

SARAH. Well he was disappointed. I've been giving him blue balls for weeks.

REBECCA. Blue balls no, no. What did you overhear him say?

SARAH. Oh yeah. Well I wasn't totally sure what it meant so I don't know if it's perverted, but I'm pretty sure it was something dirty. That's why I'm so torn. Because if it wasn't dirty, I'll feel really stupid, but if it was dirty, then I don't want anything to do with this guy.

REBECCA. Right. What did he say?

SARAH. Okay, okay. So yesterday, I met him for lunch in the student center. I was with him and three of his lacrosse buddies. So we're all eating and I excused myself to go to the bathroom. About five seconds later I realized that I left my bag at the table. So I start walking back to get it and I get to the doorway of the room and I can hear him and his buddies talking. And one of his buddies said, "so tonight's the night, huh?" And Anthony says "Yep. She's coming to my room and I'm making her dinner." Then his other buddy says, "What's on the menu?" And Anthony says, "First...." Oh God. I can't believe I'm going to say this.

REBECCA. What? What did he say?

SARAH. I can't say it. I can't do it. It's sound so...

REBECCA. Would you just say it?

SARAH. Okay. Give me a second.

REBECCA. Come on.

(**SARAH** *takes a long deep breath.*)

SARAH. He said..."First I'm going to feed her the sauseeege."

REBECCA. Feed you the sausage?

SARAH. No. The sauseeege.

REBECCA. Sauseeege? Did he say anything else?

SARAH. Yes. Then he said, "After I feed her the sauseeege, it's time for dessert. And dessert will be...vertical smile."

REBECCA. Oh my God.

SARAH. That's perverted, right?

REBECCA. Do you want me to be completely honest with you?

SARAH. Yes.

REBECCA. It's not that big a deal. He was just telling his buddies that he was expecting you to give him a blow job and then he was going to return the favor by eating you out.

SARAH. That's it?

REBECCA. That's it.

SARAH. I knew it, I knew it. You know for a second I was hoping that he was just talking about dinner and making me a sausage but I know he knows I'm a vegetarian, but then again, he's Italian and you know how it is with those people. Maybe he made me sausage anyway. Or vegetarian sausage.

REBECCA. Well he certainly planned on feeding you one.

SARAH. Rebecca!

REBECCA. Sorry. Sorry. But what did you think vertical smile was?

SARAH. Well I thought it was that but I don't know. Maybe it was a dessert. I mean, lady fingers and tiramisu kind of sound perverted too, don't they?

REBECCA. I guess but...vertical smile...well I can see how that confused you. It is a weird way to say vagina.

SARAH. I know. It's gross.

(**SARAH** *lays her head in her lap.*)

REBECCA. If you really think about it, it doesn't really look like a smile. It looks like a papaya or a passion fruit or something.

SARAH. That's gross too.

REBECCA. Well all those words for vagina are gross. What idiot came up with pussy, bush, clam, coochie, furburger, cookie, kitten, muff, poonani or pink taco... that must be Mexican.

SARAH. Are you done?

REBECCA. Yes. Sorry. That's it.

SARAH. Yes. That is it.

REBECCA. What do you mean?

SARAH. I am breaking it off with him. I want to lose my virginity to someone special not some adolescent pervert.

REBECCA. Good luck then because you're never going to get laid.

SARAH. Excuse me. Are you crazy?

REBECCA. Me? You're the one who's going to break up with this really cute, nice guy because you found out that he wants to have sex with you.

SARAH. No, he –

REBECCA. Well, a certain kind of sex I should say. Is that the problem, you don't want to do oral sex?

SARAH. Oral sex is fine, it is how he said it and who he said it to –

REBECCA. I know, you're upset because you overheard him telling his buddies how badly he wants to have sex and other stuff with you.

SARAH. Vertical smile, Rebecca! Vertical smile! Feeding me his sauseeege! That's disgusting.

REBECCA. Sarah! You do know what species you're dealing with right? He has the handicap of being male which means when all the blood rushes to the little head the bigger head gets stuck on stupid and they say the most revolting things.

SARAH. They should have a little more self control.

REBECCA. They can't. And if you want to contribute to the population of the human race then you're going to have learn to speak their language.

SARAH. This is nuts.

REBECCA. Sarah, listen to me. The second a guy meets you, he imagines you naked and he thinks about doing all sorts of sexual things with you. Then with no intelligent way to communicate these things to you, he has no choice but to run and tell his stupid little buddies about it.

SARAH. You know, it would have been fine if he had told his stupid little buddies, "Hey, guys, I'm making her dinner tonight and then ...I'm going to make love to her".

REBECCA. Yeah right.

SARAH. What's that supposed to mean?

REBECCA. Well that is what he said, only in "man talk."

SARAH. Man talk? What the fuck is man talk? That's the most idiotic thing to come out of your mouth yet.

REBECCA. I thought I just explained this to you. I didn't make this up. They write books on this. Men have been talking like this since probably the caveman era and not much has changed so you better get used to it.

SARAH. I'm not going to get used to someone being so rude and disrespectful especially considering we're dating. He –

REBECCA. Sarah –

SARAH. He was rude, he was crude –

REBECCA. Sarah –

SARAH. And he clearly has no respect –

REBECCA. Sarah, he likes you. And sometimes the more a guy likes you, the dirtier his thoughts will be. And because most men don't have filters they just kind of vomit out what they're thinking and don't realize someone may get offended.

SARAH. Oh come on.

REBECCA. Sarah, it's not like it is in the movies.

SARAH. I know it's not like the movies but guys can still be romantic and not be perverted.

REBECCA. No. Not really.

SARAH. What do you mean?

REBECCA. When a guy tells you that he wants to have you over and make you a candlelit dinner, that's code for "I want to fuck your brains out."

SARAH. I'm sure there are some guys who don't think that way.

REBECCA. Yes and they're gay. But then again, gay men would just want to do all those things to other men so...there you go.

SARAH. So you're telling me that all guys are perverts?

REBECCA. I'm telling you that all people are perverts. Women too.

SARAH. You're insane.

REBECCA. Oh please. You know I'm so tired of hearing that men are so much more perverted than women. It's crap. They fantasize about sex, so do we. We may express it differently but we are by no means without our own naughty thoughts. For example weren't you planning on having sex with this guy?

SARAH. Yes.

REBECCA. Which means you thought about it before hand, right?

SARAH. Of course.

REBECCA. And it means that you probably imagined yourself riding him cowgirl style or reverse cowgirl style and you imagined his hands on your little boobies and you imagined him spanking you and –

SARAH. That is not what I imagined.

REBECCA. What the hell did you imagine?

SARAH. Not that.

REBECCA. Fine. Even if you only imagined it missionary position with you both cumming at the same time just like in the movies, it's –

SARAH. You're disgusting!

REBECCA. Okay. Fine. I'm disgusting. But why is it okay for you to have a fantasy about him but when he fantasizes about you it's wrong?

SARAH. You're not listening. Sex is fine but what he said and the way he said it is –

REBECCA. The way they talk! And you know what, sex is not fine. Sex is great. And it's fantastic when you're with the right guy and Anthony may just be that guy.

SARAH. Well I guess we'll never find out.

REBECCA. Give him a break, please. He's a guy and he can't help it. He's genetically predisposed to being a pervert. And I hate to break it to you, honey, but it won't be long until you're a pervert too.

SARAH. Oh no.

REBECCA. Oh yes.

SARAH. No way. No guy ever has to worry about overhearing me say, "Oooh, I can't wait to suck his dick and bang him so hard his dad will feel it."

REBECCA. That's it.

SARAH. What's it?

REBECCA. That's it. That's all you got to say.

SARAH. What?

REBECCA. Say it again.

SARAH. No. I'm not going to say it. It's disgusting.

REBECCA. Just do it.

SARAH. *(Mocking her)* I can't wait to suck his dick and then bang him so hard his dad will feel it.

REBECCA. No. Come on. Say it like you mean it.

SARAH. *(Exaggerated)* I can't wait to suck his dick and then bang him so hard his dad will feel it.

REBECCA. That was terrible. Let's do a little exercise here. Alright. Now, pretend I'm him.

SARAH. This is stupid.

REBECCA. Look at my rippling muscles, my green eyes, and the candles and I'm making you dinner. And I'm sweet and I'm nice and I smell good and I'm hot and I'm an athlete and I want you. Now what are you going to do to me?

(**SARAH** *grabs* **REBECCA**'s *hands, looks her in the eyes, takes a breath and makes a serious attempt...*)

SARAH. I can't wait to suck your dick and bang you so hard your dad will feel it. Oh Jesus.

REBECCA. No. Jesus would never do those things. How do you feel?

SARAH. I feel gooey.

REBECCA. It's not gooey. When you lose your virginity, you will see that this sort of thing is not offensive at all. Like I said, it's just man talk. It's the way they let you know they are attracted to you. It's like marking their territory.

SARAH. Why doesn't he just go for gold and pee on my leg?

REBECCA. Be careful what you wish for, fetishes are a whole other conversation.

SARAH. Okay. Okay. You've made your point.

REBECCA. Good. I'm glad you get it.

SARAH. I get it, but I don't like it.

REBECCA. Regardless, my virgin protegé, now it's time for you to enjoy dinner and dessert.

SARAH. Oh yeah. And it's time for you to go and eat Ronnie's sauseeege.

REBECCA. It is. And it's time for you to call Anthony and get that poke in your vertical smile.

SARAH. Well, why don't you go find yourself a vibrator and poke your own?

REBECCA. I will. I'll borrow your mother's, it has an anal probe.

(**REBECCA** and **SARAH** smile at each other.)

REBECCA & SARAH. She needs it.

REBECCA. Oh, here comes Ronnie.

SARAH. I'm out of here.

REBECCA. No. Stay for lunch.

SARAH. I don't think I can stomach it.

REBECCA. Okay. Suit yourself.

SARAH. Love you.

REBECCA. Love you too.

(They hug.

RONNIE, eating a hot dog and carrying two paper bags, returns to the stage as **SARAH** leaves.)

RONNIE. (mouth full) Sarah, where are you going? I got you a bun with ketchup.

REBECCA. Forget her.

RONNIE. Is everything okay?

REBECCA. Everything's fine. She was upset because she

overheard some guy she likes talking "dirty" about her. She doesn't understand that you guys are like that.

RONNIE. Don't all girls know that?

REBECCA. Some young girls still believe that there are men out there that don't want sex all the time. And they also think those guys are worth having.

RONNIE. And they're vegetarians.

(**RONNIE** *hands her one of the paper bags.* **REBECCA** *takes out the hot dog and starts eating it.*)

REBECCA. I love these. They always taste so good coming from those street vendors.

RONNIE. Yeah. You just can't duplicate the taste.

(**RONNIE** *finishes his hot dog, crumples up the bag and takes a shot at the trash can. He makes the shot. Or not.*

While **REBECCA** *eats,* **RONNIE** *creeps up behind the bench. He begins kissing her neck while she eats.*)

REBECCA. Ohh. You won't even wait until I'm done, will you?

RONNIE. I can't. I'm a guy, remember? Besides, food makes me hot.

REBECCA. Oh yeah? Got some thoughts running through your head?

RONNIE. Oh yeah.

(*He starts getting real serious with that neck. He giving slower kisses. She continues to eat, but she's enjoying those kisses.*)

REBECCA. You got some dirty thoughts?

RONNIE. You have no idea.

REBECCA. Yes I do. I'm an adult.

RONNIE. That's right.

REBECCA. So what are you envisioning?

RONNIE. Oh. Something real, real...hot.

REBECCA. Such as?

RONNIE. I'm envisioning something like what we've got

right here. Except you're not on a bench, you're in my bedroom. And you're not wearing those clothes, you're wearing –

REBECCA. Nothing?

RONNIE. Oh yeah. And that's not a hot dog in your mouth. You know what it is. And then I pull it out and give you a dousing.

(**REBECCA** *starts coughing.*)

RONNIE. Are you okay?

(**REBECCA** *keeps coughing. She gets up and runs over to the trash. She spits all the food out into it.*)

RONNIE. Oh my God. You're choking.

(*He runs to her and smacks her on the back. She pushes him away.*)

REBECCA. Don't touch me. Now finish what you were saying.

RONNIE. Drink some water first.

REBECCA. Finish. You were saying it's your "what" in my mouth? And what were you planning to douse me with?

(*pointing what's left of the hot dog in his face like a gun*)

RONNIE. Well, you know. It's my... you know...

REBECCA. In my mouth? And then on my face?

RONNIE. Well, yeah. That's not okay?

REBECCA. This is what you fantasize about?

RONNIE. Fantasize? We did just about everything this weekend.

REBECCA. You didn't douse anything on my face this weekend.

RONNIE. Well we put it on your chest and your stomach and you even swallowed. I didn't think that would be a big deal.

REBECCA. Not a big deal? Not a big deal?

RONNIE. Well. I don't know. I don't see... (*Flipping out*)

What? What's wrong?

REBECCA. You're a fucking degenerate.

RONNIE. Are you insane? Did you suddenly turn into Sarah?

REBECCA. I didn't know you're idea of romance was imagining me on my knees submitting to your every whim and then taking a... taking a...dousing. Oh you're disgusting!

(*She realizes she's still holding the hot dog and she tosses it across the stage in disgust*)

RONNIE. I can't believe this. After the way we did things this weekend.

REBECCA. I can't believe I did all that stuff with you. I must be getting dumber as I get older.

RONNIE. Yeah. You and me both.

REBECCA. Oh my God. Why can't you be like a normal guy –

RONNIE. A normal guy? Okay.

REBECCA. Why can't you just fantasize about a threesome with me and my cousin or my best friend or something?

RONNIE. I did. And your mother, and your sister.

REBECCA. Yeah. And I bet you imagined us all on our knees.

RONNIE. You got it.

(**RONNIE** *grunts three times as he makes a motion to the ground as if three women are on their knees for him and they're all giving him head.*)

REBECCA. You make me sick.

RONNIE. I don't get you.

REBECCA. And you never will again.

RONNIE. Great. So we're through? Just like that?

REBECCA. You got that right. I'm not spending another minute with...with...

RONNIE. A guy?

REBECCA. No. A guy like you.

RONNIE. Why don't you run and go catch your cousin and go complain about me?

REBECCA. Why don't you go find yourself a porn star who will live on her knees and do that...stuff!

RONNIE. I might just do that.

REBECCA. You disgust me.

RONNIE. We've covered that.

REBECCA. Well I'll say it one more time. You disgust me.

RONNIE. Why are you still standing here? Go.

REBECCA. I'm going now.

RONNIE. Go. See ya'.

REBECCA. Eat me.

RONNIE. I have.

REBECCA. Pervert.

> (**REBECCA** *storms off stage.*
>
> **RONNIE** *sits down on the bench and stretches. He reaches down for the other paper bag. He pulls out another hot dog.*
>
> *He eats. He's enjoying that hot dog. It's peaceful, serene. Just Ronnie and the hot dog.*)

RONNIE. You just can't duplicate the taste.

> (*Several moments pass as* **RONNIE** *enjoys his hot dog.* **REBECCA** *returns. He doesn't notice. She approaches him looking at the ground as if trying to gather her strength.*)

REBECCA. Oh my God. You're eating?

RONNIE. What are you doing back?

REBECCA. I was coming back to see if you would apologize. But you're eating.

RONNIE. Yeah. So?

REBECCA. You didn't even think about how much you hurt my feelings?

RONNIE. Sure I did.

REBECCA. But you don't want to apologize?

(*He places the half-eaten hot dog on the bench. He gets up off the bench. He walks up to her, really slowly and seductively.*)

RONNIE. Sure I do. I'm sorry I'm so attracted to you that I wanted you to fulfill all my sexual fantasies. And I in turn would've fulfilled yours. I don't know what came over me.

(*He wraps his arms around her from behind and kisses her neck.*)

REBECCA. Apology accepted.

(*He twirls her out as if they were dancing and pulls her back. She jumps into his arms and they head towards the ladies room.*)

(*The lights go down.*)

UNPROTECTED SEX

Cast of Characters

RACHEL: Brunette, mid twenties. East Village artist type. Very cute despite her frumpy manner of dress and her slightly dorky personality

BRIAN: Fair haired, boy-next-door, mid twenties. Very mild mannered.

JOE: Mid twenties. A real slacker type. He wears flip-flops, a hockey jersey and a backwards baseball cap.

Scene

A one bedroom apartment in Astoria, Queens.

Time

This evening.

ACT I

Scene I

(*The lights rise. The brick wall is now adorned with a window and a painting. A television sits at downstage left and a couch sits at center stage.*

A bunch of empty beer bottles sit on a snack table in front of the couch.

The entrance to the bedroom is off stage right. The entrance to the kitchen is off stage left and the entrance to the apartment is off stage left.

A hockey game is on. We can hear the broadcast.

JOE, *wearing his hockey jersey, baseball cap and flip flops, eats ice cream out of a carton.*

BRIAN *enters the room.*)

BRIAN. What the fuck are you doing? Put that back.

JOE. You said I could have some.

BRIAN. Yeah. Get yourself a bowl and eat it like a human being.

JOE. Fine. Where are the bowls?

BRIAN. Forget the bowls. Just put it back. We have to go over the rules again.

JOE. No. Let's watch the game.

BRIAN. In a minute.

JOE. But the game is on now.

BRIAN. But Rachel will be home any minute.

JOE. I'm not doing this.

(**JOE** *takes a seat on the couch.*)

BRIAN. Come on. We can go over this while we watch the

game.

JOE. Can I ask you a question?

BRIAN. No.

(**JOE** *puts his feet on the table.*)

JOE. Why did you –

BRIAN. Feet off the table.

(**JOE** *complies with the request.*)

JOE. Why did you –

(*In the middle of his question* **BRIAN** *grabs the bottles off of the table. He takes them to the kitchen.*

JOE *watches him in disbelief.*)

JOE (CONT'D). You have no manners.

BRIAN. You're the one with your feet on the table and you're leaving your empties all around.

JOE. I'm watching the game. I'll get rid of them in between periods.

BRIAN. That's not good enough tonight.

(**BRIAN** *starts scrubbing the table.*)

There's a bottle cap on the floor next to your foot. Can you get that?

(**JOE** *looks over. Sure enough, there's a bottle cap laying on the carpet.*)

JOE. Do you have eagle eyes?

BRIAN. Rachel would've seen it. That would've been ugly.

(**JOE** *places his beer on the table.*)

Coaster! Coaster!

JOE. This table is a piece of shit. Rachel knows it.

BRIAN. She won't care tonight.

JOE. Alright. If things are so fucking hectic, why did you have me over?

BRIAN. She knows you come over every Tuesday to watch hockey. If you didn't come tonight she'd know that I told you not to come because of her and that would get her upset.

JOE. So instead, you invite me over and I have to live with the constant fear that she's going to throw a tantrum.

BRIAN. Which brings me back to the rules. Let's go over them one more time.

JOE. I'm out of here.

> (**JOE** *gets up and heads to the door.*
>
> **BRIAN** *runs to get in front of him.*)

BRIAN. Fuck you. You're going nowhere.

> (**BRIAN** *stands in his way.*)

JOE. I can get past you.

BRIAN. I'm not dealing with this alone.

JOE. Let me out.

BRIAN. Sit down and let's go over the rules. Please.

> (**JOE** *relents. He mopes his way back towards the couch.*)

JOE. Are you sure you're not the one on the pill?

BRIAN. Just sit down.

> (*They sit on the couch.*)

BRIAN. Alright. What's the first rule?

JOE. I feel like a child.

BRIAN. Just say it.

JOE. Fine.

> (**JOE** *takes a crumpled up piece of paper out of his pocket. He opens it.*)

BRIAN. What is that?

JOE. The rules.

BRIAN. You wrote them down?

JOE. Yeah.

> (**BRIAN** *grabs it and tears it up.*)

JOE. What are you doing?

BRIAN. If she finds this she'll flip out. I'm destroying the evidence.

JOE. How do you expect me to remember the rules now?

BRIAN. Stop acting like a retard and give me rule number one.

JOE. Fine. Rule number one, be nice.

BRIAN. You can handle that. Now number two.

JOE. Agree with anything she says. No matter how absurd.

BRIAN. Good. Next one.

JOE. Don't say anything about her body. Don't even compliment her.

BRIAN. Unless...

JOE. Unless she asks for a compliment.

BRIAN. Very good.

JOE. This is the stupidest thing I've ever been involved in.

BRIAN. Me too. And what's the last rule?

JOE. Under no circumstances am I to tell her that I know about this situation.

BRIAN. And I'm going to add one more.

JOE. Let's watch the game.

BRIAN. Don't tell any of your jokes to her.

JOE. Why? She likes them. Maybe they'll cheer her up.

BRIAN. No. She'll be offended. Trust me.

JOE. So basically, the overall rule is no fun.

BRIAN. Exactly. No fun. My life isn't fun. So you don't get to have any fun. Now let's watch the game.

(**BRIAN** *turns up the volume.*)

What the fuck? When did we fall behind?

JOE. Probably when you were giving me the rules.

BRIAN. Alright. Shut up.

JOE. Can I ask you something?

BRIAN. What?

JOE. Is this all worth it?

BRIAN. It will be.

JOE. I don't think so.

BRIAN. We're going to start having unprotected sex.

JOE. Her idea or yours?

BRIAN. Ours. We both got tested for diseases and now she's on the pill.

JOE. Which is making her unbearable, undesirable and completely unattractive.

BRIAN. It's only temporary.

JOE. You hope.

BRIAN. I PRAY that it's only temporary. I swear to God, you're not going to believe what you see.

JOE. I will. She's always been kind of moody.

BRIAN. Yeah. She's always been kind of moody but now she's all over the place. She'll be smiling and joking and then she'll be crying and then she'll be pissed off. And that's just the first minute.

JOE. So we're not really going to get to watch any of this game are we?

BRIAN. Just stick to the rules and we should be okay. Hopefully she'll be so tired when she comes in that she'll just go to sleep.

JOE. But we'll have to be quiet. We won't even be able to yell after a goal.

BRIAN. We're adults. I think we can be calm.

(*They resume watching television. They lean in a bit.*

The hockey broadcaster is getting excited.)

HOCKEY BROADCASTER (O.S.) He shoots and scores!

BRIAN. Yeah!

JOE. There it is!

(*They jump up from the couch in celebration.*)

BRIAN. That was beautiful.

(*We hear someone struggling with the door.*)

RACHEL (O.S.) Open the door!

(*She BANGS on the door.*)

BRIAN. Oh shit!

(*He runs over.*)

JOE. You blew it already.

BRIAN. Shut up.

(*He runs off stage. We hear him opening a door.*

RACHEL, *wearing baggy jeans and a vest over her button down shirt, enters, followed by* **BRIAN**.)

BRIAN. Hey, Rachel.

RACHEL. Why do you have the chain lock on? Two grown men are that scared of intruders?

BRIAN. It's Joe. He's a big baby.

JOE. Yeah.

(*She laughs. She kisses* **BRIAN** *on the lips, then kisses* **JOE** *on the cheek.* **JOE** *pays her no mind and watches the game.*)

RACHEL. How was your day, sweetie?

BRIAN. It was okay. And yours?

RACHEL. Check this out. You're not going to believe this.

(*She puts her bag down on the couch and takes off her black vest. She tightens up her clothes and stands straight up, sticking her chest out.*)

Do you notice anything?

BRIAN. What am I looking for?

RACHEL. Joe, do you notice anything?

JOE. (*not looking at her*) That's a really nice outfit.

RACHEL. Oh my God. What is wrong with you two?

She starts unbuttoning her shirt.

BRIAN. What are you doing?

RACHEL. I want you to see this.

(*She takes off her shirt. She is spilling out of her bra.*)

Look what's happened to me. They're huge.

(*Out of the corner of his eye,* **JOE** *spots her. He does a* *double take.*)

JOE. Yeah those are pretty big.

RACHEL. They're heavy too. I'm not sure whether I like this or not.

(*She grabs them again.*)

Oh and they hurt. They're swelling. And my nipples are so sensitive.

(*She keeps playing with them.*)

And this bra hurts too. This bra is a C. It wasn't meant for these.

(*She pops off the bra.*)

BRIAN. Sweetheart, Joe is here.

(**BRIAN** *frantically points at* **JOE**.

She doesn't seem to notice. She covers her breasts with her hands, in awe of the size of them. She's in her own world.

JOE *can't believe what he is seeing. He is dumfounded by her chest.*

BRIAN *shakes his head.*)

BRIAN. Why don't you put your shirt back on and watch the hockey game with us?

(*She's not listening. She's fixated on her chest.* **JOE**, *trying not to laugh, looks over at* **BRIAN**. **BRIAN** *mouths, "Shut up."*)

RACHEL. Do you believe these?

BRIAN. Maybe you should put your shirt back on now.

RACHEL. I don't care if he sees them. They're not mine.

JOE. I like them.

RACHEL. Seriously?

JOE. Hell yeah!

RACHEL. Brian?

BRIAN. Of course I like them.

RACHEL. Do you like them better this way or the other

way?

(**BRIAN** *steps in front of her so* **JOE** *can no longer see.*

JOE *moves around trying to peer around him.*)

BRIAN. I like them either way.

RACHEL. But you have to have a preference.

BRIAN. I don't. They were nice before and now they're nice now.

RACHEL. They're big now.

JOE. They're beautiful. I think we should keep them.

(*She laughs.*)

RACHEL. We? You're funny. I'm going to go change.

(*She grabs her shirt and exits into the bedroom.*

JOE *starts laughing.*)

JOE. "I don't care if he sees them. They're not mine."

BRIAN. Having fun?

JOE. Believe it or not, I am. I don't think I've ever seen her so happy.

BRIAN. I can't believe she just did that.

JOE. Why do you care? They're not hers.

BRIAN. Shut the fuck up.

JOE. Don't yell at me. You could've put a stop to that.

BRIAN. There's nothing I could've done. If I tried to stop her, it would've been worse!

JOE. Alright, enough. Relax. They're just breasts. I've seen many in my life. Big deal if I see hers.

BRIAN. Yeah maybe you're right. Right now I'm just glad she's manageable. Let's keep it that way. And I will tell you one more time because you didn't listen. Do not, I repeat, do not joke with her.

JOE. I made her laugh.

BRIAN. We got lucky. I'll tell you what, when she comes back out here, just give her one word answers to whatever she says to you.

RACHEL (O.S.) Brian! Can you come here for a minute?

BRIAN. I'll be right there!

JOE. Go before she gets mad.

BRIAN. Shut the fuck up and watch the game.

JOE. I'd like to.

> (**BRIAN** *leaves the room.* **JOE** *settles in and watches the game.*
>
> *We can hear* **BRIAN** *and* **RACHEL** *arguing about something off stage.*
>
> **JOE** *turns the volume of the TV up.*
>
> *The arguing can still be heard.*)

RACHEL (O.S.) No. I don't trust you. I think you're lying.

> (**RACHEL** *charges back into the room. She's wearing a long night shirt.*
>
> **JOE** *doesn't notice her. He keeps watching the game.*
>
> **BRIAN** *comes back into the room.*)

RACHEL. Joe, turn around. Can you do me a favor?

JOE. Of course.

BRIAN. This isn't necessary.

RACHEL. I have underwear on. Shut up. Does my butt look big to you?

> (*She turns around and lifts the shirt.*)

Tell me. Does it look big?

JOE. It looks great.

RACHEL. How could it? If my tits are getting bigger, there needs to be a trade off. It's bigger I can tell.

JOE. No. It looks great.

RACHEL. Are you sure?

BRIAN. Honey, I told you. It looks great.

JOE. Yeah. Even if it was bigger, that's not a bad thing.

> (**JOE** *turns around to watch the game.* **RACHEL** *stares at him.* **BRIAN** *is about to explode on* **JOE**.)

RACHEL. What?

JOE. Huh?

RACHEL. What are you saying?

JOE. Nothing. It looks great.

RACHEL. You said "even if it was bigger."

JOE. Yeah.

RACHEL. So...

JOE. So nothing.

BRIAN. He meant that –

RACHEL. Let him say what he means.

JOE. It just means that you shouldn't worry about all this.

RACHEL. No. You're saying that my ass is flat. I know it is. I have an Irish ass. I hate it.

(*She leaves the room.*)

BRIAN. What the fuck did I tell you?

JOE. What did I do?

BRIAN. One word answers. That's all you needed to do. But no, you had to say "even if it was." Don't you know never to say that to a woman. What the fuck is the matter with you?

JOE. I'm sorry. I didn't expect to come over here and have your girlfriend showing me all her bits and pieces. She's a hot chick and it scrambled my brain a bit!

(**JOE** *gets up in his face.*)

BRIAN. Alright. Alright. I'm sorry.

JOE. Okay. I'm sorry too.

BRIAN. Let's forget it. Let's just watch the game.

JOE. I'd like that.

(*They sit back down and watch the game. They raise the volume of the game.*

RACHEL *comes out of the bedroom again, this time wearing sweatpants.*)

RACHEL. I'm sorry, guys. I shouldn't have snapped like that.

BRIAN. You didn't snap. It's okay.

JOE. Yeah. It's okay.

RACHEL. I just had a terrible day and I think I took it out on you guys a little.

BRIAN. What happened? Do you want to talk about it?

RACHEL. No. But can I watch the game with you guys?

BRIAN. Of course.

(**JOE** *moves over a bit to make room. She sits in between them. She leans on* **BRIAN** *and cuddles with him.*)

RACHEL. Who's playing?

BRIAN. The Islanders and the Oilers.

RACHEL. Who's winning?

BRIAN. It's tied.

(Beat.)

RACHEL. Joe, how's your life?

JOE. Good.

RACHEL. Just good?

JOE. Good.

RACHEL. Do you have a girlfriend?

JOE. No.

RACHEL. How come?

(*He shrugs his shoulders.*)

You don't know?

JOE. No.

RACHEL. Are you upset at me?

JOE. No.

RACHEL. Are you sure?

JOE. Yeah.

RACHEL. Why won't you talk to me?

BRIAN. He takes the game very serious.

RACHEL. Don't you think that's childish?

JOE. Yeah.

RACHEL. Alright. He's pissed at me.

JOE. No.

RACHEL. Can you answer one of my questions then with something besides a no or yes?

JOE. Yes.

RACHEL. Okay. You're not funny.

(**JOE** *starts laughing.*)

What are you laughing at?

BRIAN. Forget him.

RACHEL. Why won't he talk to me?

BRIAN. Joe, just answer her questions.

JOE. Are you sure?

RACHEL. What is wrong with you two?

JOE. Nothing. I'm sorry. I'm very immature. When I get into the game I can't concentrate on anything else.

RACHEL. That's probably why you don't have a girlfriend.

JOE. I think you're right.

(*They all return their attention to the TV.*)

RACHEL. I hope the Islanders win. I like them. I hooked up with an Islander when I was in college.

JOE. Really?

RACHEL. He had all these scars on his face. He was sexy. But that was before I met this gorgeous cutie.

(*She kisses* **BRIAN**.)

JOE. He is gorgeous.

RACHEL. God, I miss those days. I had sex without worry.

JOE. Tell me about it.

RACHEL. Stop it. You're still there.

JOE. No I'm not.

RACHEL. Yes you are. You don't have a girlfriend.

JOE. Exactly. So I have to worry about diseases.

RACHEL. Oh please. Do you know how hard it is for a guy to get HIV if he wears a condom?

JOE. There are other diseases out there.

RACHEL. Fine. But you don't have to worry about getting pregnant.

JOE. But I can get a girl pregnant.

RACHEL. It's not the same.

JOE. It's similar.

RACHEL. But it's not the same. You can walk away. A woman can't.

JOE. I can't walk away. I'm a stand up guy.

RACHEL. But you CAN. A woman can't.

JOE. A woman has choices.

RACHEL. Oh right. And they're very desirable ones too.

JOE. It's still choices.

BRIAN. Alright, Joe. Shut up. Enough.

JOE. You know what, Rachel? You're right. It isn't the same.

RACHEL. Don't patronize me. If you don't agree, state your opinion.

JOE. Well, I did.

RACHEL. Fine.

JOE. Fine.

(*They return their attention to the TV.* **RACHEL** *lays back down on Brian's chest. She is seething.*

She jumps off his chest.)

RACHEL. The fact that you can even suggest that you have the same amount of worries when it comes to sex as we do is amazing. Just think about it for a second. We're more likely to catch diseases, but we're less likely to have an orgasm. We're capable of multiple orgasms, but no guys know how to take us there. Then we're the ones who have to take the birth control drugs which fuck up our moods, then you hate us. We have to have our periods every month, you guys have nothing like that. Then when it's time to have a baby, we carry it around, get fat, squeeze the thing out and go through all that pain while you just wait for us to slim back down again so you can bang us again. Then we have to breast feed these things and that hurts and it makes our breasts saggy. Then as the kids stress us out and we gain weight, you get less attracted to us and leave us for some young piece of ass who hasn't dealt with gravity yet. You guys get all the fun parts. So basically, we get to take all the precautions and you guys get to stick it in and leave whenever you want.

JOE. Yeah. And I'm going to get myself another beer. Can I get you one, Rachel?

RACHEL. No you can't because I don't want anything else messing with my head. I can't take this anymore. It's only been a few days and I'm flipping out. I don't ever want to have sex again because I hate it. You understand me? I hate it! I hate it! I hate it!

(*She starts crying and heads for the bedroom.* **BRIAN** *runs after her.*

She disappears into the bedroom. **BRIAN** *goes right in after her.*

She comes right back out of the bedroom followed by **BRIAN**.)

RACHEL. I'm sorry.

BRIAN. It's okay. Just relax. Breathe.

(**JOE** *and* **BRIAN** *mimic breathing exercises.*)

RACHEL. I'm sorry, Joe. I'm acting crazy. I'm on the pill and it's messing up my moods something terrible.

JOE. Oh. I didn't know.

RACHEL. It would have been nice for you tell him, Brian. I don't want him to think I'm psycho.

BRIAN. I thought you might want to keep it private.

RACHEL. Then you shouldn't have had him over. You guys also don't think much do you?

JOE. You're right. We don't.

RACHEL. Alright. I'm going to stop. I'm sorry.

(*She wipes the tears from her eyes.*)

No more crying. It's just that...oww.

(*She has some kind of pain in her breasts as she clutches them.*)

I'm going to bed.

(*She storms out of the room.*)

JOE. Wow.

BRIAN. I told you.

JOE. Thank God that's over. Is that it?

BRIAN. I hope so. Let's hope she falls right asleep.

JOE. You go through this every night?

BRIAN. The past few.

JOE. Damn. It's a sad state of affairs when a man's main goal in life is to get his girlfriend to go to sleep.

BRIAN. Alright. Let's watch the game.

(**BRIAN** *grabs the remote and turns the volume back up. They settle back in on the couch and watch the TV.*)

JOE. Just for future reference, your advice sucks. I go with the one word answer thing and it almost fucks everything up.

BRIAN. That was a bad idea.

JOE. You yelled at me twice tonight.

BRIAN. I lost my temper.

JOE. Yes you did. Apologize.

BRIAN. We'll talk later.

JOE. Apologize to me.

BRIAN. I'm sorry.

JOE. Alright.

BRIAN. Let's watch the game.

(*They settle back in and watch the TV.*

RACHEL *comes out of the bedroom again. She walks past the couch and heads straight for the kitchen.*)

BRIAN. Everything okay, honey?

RACHEL. I want ice cream.

(**RACHEL** *comes out of the kitchen with a carton of ice cream. She holds it over her head.*)

RACHEL. Who finished this?

BRIAN. What do you mean?

RACHEL. What do you mean what do I mean? Somebody put an empty carton of ice cream in the freezer.

BRIAN. I don't eat ice cream.

RACHEL. Well somebody did. And who the hell would put an empty carton of ice cream in the freezer?

JOE. I'm sorry. I did that.

RACHEL. You? Why would you do something like that?

(*She storms back into the kitchen.*)

BRIAN. I told you not to finish it.

JOE. I wasn't paying attention to what I was doing.

RACHEL (O.S.) All I wanted was to have some ice cream and go to bed and not only is there none left but an empty carton is in there just to tease me.

JOE. I'll run down and get you some.

(**JOE** *gets up and heads to the door.*)

RACHEL (O.S.) No.

JOE. It's really no problem. I'll do it.

BRIAN. Go right now.

JOE. I'm out.

RACHEL (O.S.) Don't bother.

JOE. I'm going.

RACHEL (O.S.) I said no.

JOE. I'll be back before you know it.

(*She storms back in and shoves* **JOE** *back towards the couch.*)

RACHEL. I won't eat it. Even if Tom Carvel showed up at the door with a fucking soft serve machine I wouldn't eat ice cream now.

(*She storms back into the kitchen.* **JOE** *returns to the couch.*

RACHEL *comes out of the kitchen with two handfuls of beer bottles.*)

RACHEL. Why are these in the trash? These are recyclable.

BRIAN. I was just trying to keep the place clean.

RACHEL. But you can't do it right can you? But why would you care as long as you're getting what you want right? I hope you don't expect me to clean all these dishes. And, Joe, you better clean up your fucking mess because I'm in no mood to clean up after you. I already live with one child and I'm not interested in cleaning up after another one. I can't wait to see what the bathroom looks like. Did either of you piss all over the seat and not wipe it up? Did you put the toilet seat down? Is there water all over the sink? Fuck!

(*She puts the bottles down on the table and storms off stage into the bedroom.*

BRIAN *looks defeated.*

JOE *laughs.*)

BRIAN. What the fuck are you laughing at?

JOE. You know what this is like? It's like when we were kids and we were trying to play wiffle ball and the wind would kick up and we'd have to stop. Then the wind would die down and we'd play a little bit, then the wind would kick up again and we'd have to stop again. That's what this is like.

BRIAN. Shut the fuck up.

JOE. She's like a human storm.

BRIAN. That was your fault.

JOE. I didn't put the bottles in the garbage.

BRIAN. And you didn't put the ice cream in the garbage either.

JOE. It was both our faults.

BRIAN. You set her off.

JOE. Enough. Let's watch the game.

BRIAN. You're right. You know what? This is none of our faults. Not even hers. It's the drugs.

(**RACHEL** *comes back into the room. She's wearing a*

different outfit. She has different sweatpants and a different tee shirt on.)

RACHEL. I'm sorry that I was being a bitch, you guys.

JOE. It's okay.

(**BRIAN** *slaps* **JOE** *in the chest.*)

BRIAN. You weren't being a bitch, baby.

RACHEL. I overreacted to all that stuff. I'm sorry, Joe. Do you forgive me?

JOE. Of course.

RACHEL. Brian, do you forgive me?

BRIAN. There's nothing to forgive.

RACHEL. It's just that I had this awful day.

BRIAN. Well come over here. Tell us about it this time.

(*She heads for the couch.*)

BRIAN. Did you change your clothes?

(*She stops right in Joe's view of the game.* **JOE** *tries to look around her to see the TV but to no avail.*)

RACHEL. Yes. I looked like a pig in that.

BRIAN. No you didn't.

RACHEL. Yes I did and do you want to hear what happened to me at work today?

BRIAN. Yes.

JOE. Absolutely.

(**JOE** *still can't see around her. He grabs her by the hips and pulls her down onto the couch.*

BRIAN *kisses her on the cheek.*)

BRIAN. I love you. Look, we'll even shut off the game.

(**BRIAN** *shuts the game off.* **JOE** *throws his hands in the air in frustration.* **BRIAN** *waves him off behind her back.*)

Come on tell us about it. What happened at work today?

RACHEL. Well, it wasn't what happened at work. That was bad. But it was really what happened on the subway on the way home.

BRIAN. Did somebody bother you?

RACHEL. No.

BRIAN. Did you have to stand?

RACHEL. No.

BRIAN. What is it?

RACHEL. There was this group of kids. They were teenagers and there was this one retarded boy on the train. And...

(*She starts to cry.* **BRIAN** *puts his arm around her.*)

All the teenagers started making fun of the retarded boy.

(*She becomes a little more hysterical.* **BRIAN** *pulls her close to him.*)

It was so mean. And all I could thinks was, how could anyone be so mean? And that poor boy. He goes home, and those kids make fun of him but they're okay. They go out and have fun and live a great life while that poor retarded boy goes the rest of his life getting made fun of.

BRIAN. Relax, relax.

(*She buries her head in his shoulders.* **JOE** *is visibly frustrated and motions for* **BRIAN** *to turn on the TV.* **BRIAN** *waves him off.*)

It's okay. They're just kids.

RACHEL. That's no excuse.

BRIAN. I know it's no excuse, but it's what kids do.

RACHEL. I never did that when I was a kid.

BRIAN. Well, it's what boys do.

RACHEL. Boys are jerks.

BRIAN. We can be.

RACHEL. You never made fun of retarded kids did you?

BRIAN. No way. Never.

RACHEL. Are you lying?

BRIAN. No. Tell her, Joe.

RACHEL. Was he mean to retarded kids in high school?

JOE. No. He was so nice. He was a gentlemen. He bullied the bullies. He was like a freedom fighter.

RACHEL. What about you?

JOE. I never made fun of retarded people.

RACHEL. You're so sweet. I'm glad we're friends. I'm glad you're friends with Brian.

(*She kisses him on the cheek and hugs him.* JOE *looks at* BRIAN *and shrugs.*)

Thanks for letting me get that off my chest. I feel so much better.

BRIAN. Good.

RACHEL. Okay. I'm going to go to bed now.

BRIAN. Good night.

JOE. Good night.

(*She leaves the room.*)

JOE. I did good.

BRIAN. You did good.

JOE. I defended you.

BRIAN. You redeemed yourself.

JOE. Oh I'm so proud.

BRIAN. Now we can watch the game.

JOE. Yes!

(BRIAN *turns the game back on.*)

Great. We missed a goal.

BRIAN. Don't start.

(RACHEL *enters the room again, giddy and skipping around.*)

RACHEL. Can I watch the rest of the game with you guys?

BRIAN. Of course.

JOE. I thought you were going to bed.

RACHEL. I'm too fidgety.

BRIAN. Come on. Sit down.

RACHEL. Hanging out with the boys!

(*She runs to the couch and dives over them, draping her legs over* **JOE** *with no regard for his comfort. She nearly kicks the beer bottle out of his hand.*

JOE *looks over at* **BRIAN** *for some help.* **BRIAN** *waves him off again.*)

BRIAN. I think the Islanders are finally going to win one.

(**JOE** *tosses* **RACHEL**'s *legs off of him and gets up from the couch.*)

JOE. I'm going to get that beer.

RACHEL. Joe, please don't put that bottle in the garbage.

JOE. Sure. Where do you want it?

RACHEL. Put it in the sink and I'll take care of it.

JOE. Are you sure?

RACHEL. Yes. Thank you.

JOE. Can I get you something, Rachel? Water? Some chamomille tea with honey?

RACHEL. No, but thank you for asking. You're really sweet.

(**JOE** *heads for the kitchen.*

RACHEL *and* **BRIAN** *settle in.*)

JOE (O.S.) Hey, dude, where's the bottle opener?

BRIAN. It's in there.

JOE (O.S.) I don't see it.

BRIAN. Can't you use your shirt?

JOE *(Reappearing.)* I'm not going to use this shirt. Are you crazy?

BRIAN. Just look for it.

(**JOE** *leaves stage again.*)

RACHEL. Honey, help him.

BRIAN. He can find it himself. Check in the drawer!

JOE (O.S.) Not there.

BRIAN. Look in the cabinet.

JOE (O.S.) Nope.

> (**BRIAN** *leans his head back so he can see into the kitchen.*)

BRIAN. There it is. Right on the counter.

JOE (O.S.) Where?

BRIAN. Right there. By the dish rack.

JOE (O.S.) I don't see it.

BRIAN. It's right in front of your face.

JOE (O.S.) I don't see it.

RACHEL. You're giving me a headache. Just help him.

BRIAN. He can find it.

JOE (O.S.) Come on. I'm missing the game.

BRIAN. It's right there. I can see it.

JOE (O.S.) Where?

BRIAN. Right in front of your face?

JOE (O.S.) Come on, man.

BRIAN. Are you fucking retarded?

> (**RACHEL** *slowly rises from his lap.* **BRIAN** *buries his head in his hands. He's crossed the line.*
>
> **RACHEL** *hits* **BRIAN** *with a look of death.*)

RACHEL. I can't believe you just said that.

> (*He won't look at her.*)

Why are you so insensitive?

BRIAN. Just shut up. I've been listening to you all week.

> (**JOE** *returns from the kitchen.*)

JOE. If someone would just tell me where the bottle opener is, I'll leave you two alone.

RACHEL. Oh I'm sorry if this is an inconvenience for you –

BRIAN. Well it is. Just go to bed. Go in the bedroom and go

to bed.

RACHEL. Don't order me around.

BRIAN. You're feeling miserable and you're upset so do what any normal person would do and go be by yourself.

RACHEL. What is wrong with you?

BRIAN. What is wrong with me?

(**RACHEL** *looks over and sees* **JOE** *standing there waiting.*)

RACHEL. And what the fuck is the matter with you?

(*She marches into the kitchen and returns with the bottle opener.*)

RACHEL. Here it is, right in front of your eyes. How could you miss it?

(*She grabs his beer, opens it, shoves it back at him and throws the opener back at him.*)

JOE. Thank you.

(**JOE** *takes a seat on the couch and puts the game back on.*)

RACHEL. I'm breaking up with you. I hate you! I hate you so much!
You're selfish and you have stupid friends and...

(**BRIAN** *gets up from the couch, ready for the fight.* **JOE** *has never looked so happy. He's in his own world just watching the game.*)

BRIAN. I gotta be honest with you, Rachel, I can't put up with this much longer.

RACHEL. Oh you can't put up with this? You can't?

BRIAN. I don't want to talk about this in front of Joe.

RACHEL. Could you pay attention to me for five minutes please and not worry about your retarded friend?

(*She smacks* **JOE** *in the head and throws his hat onto the floor.*)

JOE. What did I do?

BRIAN. What more do you want from me? I'm trying. I don't know what the hell to say to you? One minute you're crying, next minute you're happy then you're angry. And nothing I say is the right thing.

RACHEL. You're such a little drama queen.

BRIAN. I'm the drama queen?

RACHEL. You knew all this was going to happen but you didn't seem to mind when the idea of unprotected sex came up, did you?

BRIAN. No I didn't. But now I'm at a point where I think I'd rather fuck Joe.

(*She looks at him in utter amazement.* BRIAN *looks the other way.*

JOE *is not paying any attention. He's really into the hockey game.* RACHEL *has a look that can burn through lead.*)

RACHEL. How could you say that to me? That was so mean.

(*She starts crying.*)

BRIAN. It's just, yeah, I'm sorry. All these rules and precautions and regulations. It's kind of taking the fun out of everything.

RACHEL. Like this is fun for me?

BRIAN. I know it's not fun for you, baby.

(*He tries to take her hands. She smacks them away.*)

RACHEL. Don't call me baby.

BRIAN. Fine.

RACHEL. You know, it's just what I figured. It's all about fun and games for the men right? We get all the responsibility.

BRIAN. I take responsibility.

RACHEL. You couldn't even separate the recyclables!

(*She puts her hands over her mouth, realizing she's being ridiculous.*

BRIAN *puts his hands on her shoulders.*)

RACHEL. I'm sorry. I'm sorry.

BRIAN. Alright. Relax. Calm down. We're in this together.

RACHEL. I'm such a bitch.

BRIAN. No you're not. This will all be over soon.

RACHEL. I want you to get out of the apartment and finish watching the game with Joe at a bar or something.

BRIAN. No. I want to stay with you. We're in this together.

RACHEL. No. I'm just going to keep yelling at you.

BRIAN. Are you sure?

RACHEL. Yes. Go out. Go to the bar.

BRIAN. Okay.

(**BRIAN** *trots towards the door.*)

RACHEL. Wait, wait, wait, wait.

(*She runs over to catch him.*)

RACHEL. Do you promise that you're not going to meet a twenty year old chick and leave me for her?

BRIAN. I swear.

RACHEL. Okay. Okay.

(*She smiles. He kisses her. He pulls her in for a big hug. He squeezes her.*)

Ow!

(*She pulls away from him, grasping her breasts.*)

BRIAN. I'm sorry. I' sorry.

(*She falls down onto the couch, laying her head in* **JOE***'s lap. She's still clutching her breasts.*)

RACHEL. Oh my God. I'm so tired.

(**BRIAN** *comes to the couch and rubs her temples.* **JOE** *pats her on the hip, but keeps his attention on the game.*)

RACHEL. My head is pounding.

BRIAN. Come on. Breathe.

RACHEL. I just want to go to bed.

BRIAN. You have to stay there this time.

RACHEL. I'll stay there.

BRIAN. Okay. Come on. I'll tuck you in.

(*He pulls her up off of the couch. She climbs on to him like a little kid, wrapping her legs around him.*

Her breasts get a little too close to his chest.)

RACHEL. Be careful.

BRIAN. I'm being careful.

(*He carries her towards the bedroom. She clutches her breasts in pain again.*)

RACHEL. I'm sorry I was so difficult tonight.

BRIAN. You're doing everything you can to make our relationship work and I know that. So it's okay.

RACHEL. Good night, Joe.

JOE. Good night. Feel better.

(**BRIAN** *carries her off stage into the bedroom.*

BRIAN *comes back into the living room.*)

JOE. Storm over?

BRIAN. Yeah. Let's go.

JOE. Where?

BRIAN. We're going to finish watching the game at a bar.

JOE. Okay.

BRIAN. Come on. Hurry. Before she come back out here.

(**JOE** *sprints to the door. They leave the stage and we hear the door slam off stage.*)

RACHEL (O.S.) Brian! Can you come here for a minute?

(*The stage goes dark.*)

THE MISEDUCATION OF ELISSA

Cast of Characters

ELISSA: Quirky, adorable blonde in her early twenties. Despite the bumpy road she has travelled, she maintains a glowing innocence.

Scene

Elissa's bedroom in her Brooklyn apartment.

Time

About six o'clock today.

ACT I

Scene I

(*The lights rise. The brick wall is now empty. A white, antique dresser sits upstage right. It has women's clothes hanging out of it.* **ELISSA**, *dressed in a very provocative outfit, enters from upstage left.*)

ELISSA. What do you think? Do I look okay?

(*She turns around and models her outfit.*)

I put a lot of thought into this outfit. But I'm not really sure why because in about six or seven hours it will be crumpled up on the floor as I have sex. Yes, that's right. I will be getting laid tonight. Not because I want to, I mean I guess I do, but the real reason I'm having sex tonight is because... I have to. Okay. I know it sounds strange and you're probably thinking, "what kind of self respecting woman would have sex out of obligation" but trust me, I have to. And before you judge me, which I can tell you are already doing, let me share something with you. And please bear with me because at first, this will sound a little strange.

You see, I'm in this women's psychology class right now. And we've been talking about female's and their relationship to their fathers. According to the professor and the dumb book we are reading, a woman will relate to men the way she relates to her father. In other words, if a little girl has a healthy relationship with her father, then she will have healthy relationships with men.

Now you would be hard pressed to find someone who has a better relationship to her father than me. Sure, my parents divorced when I was very young but my daddy always was there. He showed up on time every weekend to pick me up when it was his turn. He never forgot a birthday, never forgot Christmas. He bought me the nicest gifts. Every Memorial Day weekend he would take me to Great Adventure. To this day, my father has never broken a promise to me. I'm his little princess and he never fails to tell me so and he never fail to tell me how beautiful I am.

So anyway, because of my relationship with my father, I learned several things about men. One, men always keep their promises. That's a good one, right? Two, men always make you feel good about yourself. Another gem. Three, men always put you first. No comment on that one. And finally, and I guess above all, men can be trusted. Mmm. Men can be trusted. Right, right. Men can be trusted? Anyone else buy into that one?

Well I've lived most of my life believing this. Do you want to take a guess where it has gotten me?

Let's start at my sexual coming of age, shall we? Well I lost my virginity when I was sixteen to a guy who was twenty four. Sure, I knew it was illegal but he was so nice and sweet. He took me around in his car and bought me all sorts of gifts. He let me drink beer. He called me "baby." And I wrote his name in all my notebooks and all my textbooks and I was sure that he was "the one". I was sure we would get married the minute I turned eighteen. Well, it probably doesn't surprise you to know that he disappeared the minute I turned seventeen. Do you want to know why? Because I wouldn't give him a blow job. Come on. I was a kid. Remember when you were young and you found out what a blow job was? "Hello. You're going to stick THAT in my mouth? What?"

But hey, I was a good sport. I let him deflower me. Did he appreciate that? No. He got pissed off because...well, let's just say that since this was my first time, things got a bit messy. Was he sympathetic? No. He freaked out about the stain on his satin sheets. What did he expect bringing a sixteen-year-old virgin home and sticking his nine inch penis in her? Fucking son of a bitch. I should've brought him up on charges.

Okay. So. Do you think I learned my lesson from him? Of course not. I just figured, "Hey, one bad guy. No big deal." So in my senior year of high school, I started dating another older guy. He played basketball for St. John's. He was six foot five, muscular and also had a huge penis and I'm talking.

(*She uses her hand to suggest the length.*)

Anyway at least he was legal. And he was so nice too. He took me to all these college parties, introduced me to all these people, I sat right near the court for basketball games. He paid for everything. He would send flowers to me at school. He brought me balloons on my birthday. I loved him. And now that I had a better idea of what I was doing in bed, the sex was good. I had no problems doing anything now.

That is until this one night when we were messing around and he says to me, "I want to do it like they do in the pornos."

I had no idea what that meant but I trusted him. Why wouldn't I? You can trust men, right? So he tells me to close my eyes, so I do. And all of a sudden I feel something all over my face. Now I knew what it was, I wasn't stupid.

And maybe it wouldn't have been so bad if he didn't burst out laughing in this awful hyena laugh. Something about his laugh freaked me out, so I ran into the bathroom to see what he did to me. When I opened my eyes and saw my reflection in the mirror, well, I'll spare you the graphic details, but let's just say that it looked like an elephant sneezed on face.

And I don't know if you know anything about man stuff, but when it gets in your eyes, it burns! So I must have gotten some kind of infection from it and for the next few days it looked like I had pink eye and when we'd hang out he would break out laughing in that hyena laugh at random times and not tell me what he was laughing at. But I knew. So we broke up.

Okay, so two boyfriends down and did I learn my lesson? Of course not. All I learned from Blow-Job Boy and the Elephant Man is that men have large penises. So between that and my already ingrained belief that men can be trusted, I was in great shape for college, wasn't I? Well suffice it to say, college has been nothing short of a nightmare. I have dated four other men and those relationships have been nothing short of disastrous. Let's see, two of them cheated on me, one was with my cousin, who's a guy but that's another story all together.

As for the third one, well we went out a few dates and we waited until week four of our relationship to have sex. And then he never called me again. The scum bag put in four weeks just for a booty call. You know, there's actually a side of me that respects that. I don't know why.

But I have to say the fourth one was my favorite. This guy had this odd fetish. He liked to...how do I put this delicately. I'll just say it, he liked to cum on my feet.

(*She shakes her foot out.*)

Now I know what you're thinking, "Yay for you, you made the leap from the face to the feet," but you're wrong. That was really creepy. So I dumped him.

Anyway, after him, I tried the one night stand thing. And for any of you ladies out there considering the one night stand, it's a bad idea. On the night in question I was completely inebriated and I was talking to a guy who looked just like George Clooney, and I'm sticking to that. So anyway, after chatting for a bit, I said to him, "Get your shit, we're leaving." So I took him home and well I, you know, I mean, so would you, hello, George Clooney.

After our night of passion, we agreed to meet for lunch

the next day in the student center. So I'm there with my girlfriends and they all start laughing and giggling and pointing at some guy heading towards me. And whoever this guy was, he looked nothing like George Clooney. As he got closer, my heart sank as I looked at my perfect ten and saw the decimal point drift twelve spaces to the left.

After that I decided to become a lesbian. But don't get excited because it didn't last very long. When that brief experiment ended, I dusted myself off and had an epiphany. I decided I must resume my quest for the good guy. But this time, I had learned my lesson. All these guys finally got through to me. I realized that men can't be trusted and that I must take everything they say with a grain of salt. And the first guy I've met under my new mode of thinking is the guy I'm going to have sex with tonight, David.

He's a gentleman He opens doors for me. He pulls out my chair for me. He compliments me. He's protective. He treats me right. You know who he reminds me of? My father.

We went out on a few dates and had a real nice time. Well I fell right into my old trap and I slept with him sooner than I planned. But it was good. He was good. And he liked to cuddle after. So I threw it all out the window. David was making me trust again.

When he left in the morning, he said he'd call me and we'd have dinner. Oh God, I was feeling so good. I hadn't felt that good since, ever. I was falling fast and hard. Now guess what? He never called. I gave him another day. And then another. I couldn't believe that this happened to me again.

No matter what I do, I get fucked every time, no pun intended. But you know what? I wasn't going to put up with it this time. No way. It was time to fight back. I drank a lot of tequila and I called that son of a bitch. And to his credit, he answered. And I let him have it, "You son of a bitch. Who do you think you are? How dare you. I think it's pretty messed up that you just come over and sleep with me and don't call me." I stopped. There was a brief moment of silence. And he just said, "Yeah. I think it's pretty fucked up that my father dropped dead of a heart attack."

Oh. Okay. Sorry.

I cried for about three days after that. And look, I feel terrible about his dad but I still think he should have at least called or text messaged and said something.

So anyway, it's all smoothed over and he's back in town tonight and we're going out. And I have to have sex with him. I need to make it up to him and I have to give him a sympathy thing. If I don't, I'm afraid he'll leave me. And yes, I do feel bad about sleeping with a guy just to keep him around. But I think he's a good one and I've already screwed up with him and I'm afraid that if I lose him I'll be back to dating guys with freakishly large penises who have no idea where to deposit their ejaculate. So, once again, before you judge me, think how you would act if you were me.

How would you act if you had a dad who treated you like a little princess and got you to trust men, all kinds? Maybe you should consider that you are one of the lucky ones who has a dad that ignored them and maybe you learned young that men suck and they're not worth your time.

Maybe you're one of the real lucky ones like my friend Heather whose dad verbally abused her to the point where she stays away from men altogether. I can't even tell you how jealous I am of her, no men, no drama, no heartaches and, I guess no sex either, so that's no fun.

Well, speaking of which, I better get going. It's time to meet David. But before I go, let me just say one thing to all the fathers out there. I think I've figured out a solution. Do us all a favor, and stop being nice to your daughters. When they want help with their homework, just keep watching the football game. We all know that's what you want to do anyway. Go team. And when they need a shoulder to cry on, just ignore them and take that call from the office. We know it's more important. And lastly, and perhaps most important, please don't be nice to our mothers. Just lie to them and cheat on them or just do something so that we can get an idea of what is really waiting for us out there.

Do you get it? No. Of course you don't. I don't get it. You don't get it. Freud didn't get it. Who the hell can figure this shit out anyway? It doesn't matter what you have, good father, bad father, no father, my father, your father, mothers, sons, daughters, grandparents, birds, bees, giraffes, goats, midgets, and...and...and...

Oh fuck this I have to go have sex.

(*Elissa leaves the stage as the lights go down.*)

THE NUDE SCENE

Cast of Characters

JENNIFER: Early twenties, short, boy-cut hairstyle. She's a cutie. A real peacemaker type.

SPENCER: An obnoxious snobby filmmaker in his late twenties. He really thinks highly of himself. He's slightly effeminate.

KRISTOFF: Surly, grouchy camera operator in his early thirties.

KATY: A bar hopping, bed hopping vixen in her early twenties. She's hot and she knows it.

BARRY: GQ handsome actor in his late twenties. He has a great physique but he seems to lack intelligence.

Scene

Sound stage on the west side of Manhattan.

Time

Earlier today, right after lunch.

NOTE FOR PRODUCERS: The Nude Scene should be performed at a very fast pace. The piece is meant to be a farcical finale to the show and should be performed at a kinetic, rapid pace in order to get the most humor out of the chaos that is happening in the story.

ACT I

Scene I

(*The lights rise. Five pieces of red velvet hang off of a curtain rod on the brick wall.*

A couch sits at center stage. There is a small, stool in front of the couch. A movie camera sits in a camera bag at stage left.

JENNIFER, *wearing a bathrobe, stands next to the couch and does some kind of yoga-like breathing exercise. She has her hands together and raised above her head. She kicks her leg out and balances on one leg.*

She's in heavy concentration as she now stretches her left arm as far as she can, and then she replaces it with her right arm.

She lifts her arms over her head. She repeats.

She is in total meditation.

All alone.

At peace.

A perfect world for her.

KATY *creeps onto the stage. She is dressed to kill in a low-rise mini skirt and a tight top. It looks like she's looking to be discovered.*

She sees **JENNIFER** *and silently laughs to herself.*

JENNIFER *continues her breathing.*

KATY *tiptoes up to* **JENNIFER**, *hoping not to disturb her.*

Right in the middle of one of the breathing moves, **KATY** *grabs her breasts!*)

KATY. Gotcha!

(**JENNIFER** *jumps, nearly having a heart attack.*)

JENNIFER. Damnit, Katy! What is the matter with you?

KATY. I couldn't keep my hands off the big star!

(**JENNIFER** *rubs her chest a bit.*)

JENNIFER. That hurt. Why did you do that?

KATY. You look so cute doing your little Zen thing that I had to do it.

(**KATY** *starts grabbing for her again.* **JENNIFER** *smacks her hand away.*)

JENNIFER. Get off of me!

KATY. Oh my God. You're in a mood.

JENNIFER. Of course I am. You're a half hour late and you're making me look bad.

KATY. I'm sorry. I hit traffic.

(**JENNIFER** *adjusts her robe, giving a quick flash of her outfit to* **KATY.**)

KATY. Wait. What was that?

JENNIFER. What was what?

KATY. What are you wearing under that robe?

JENNIFER. It's my costume.

KATY. Let me see.

JENNIFER. Are you going to laugh at me?

KATY. I just want to see it.

JENNIFER. I swear to God, Katy. If you laugh...

KATY. Just show me.

JENNIFER. Okay.

(**JENNIFER** *opens her robe. She's wearing the most ridiculous outfit. It's a black corset replete with garter belts and fishnet stockings, which have holes in them and five-inch heels with pink puffs on them. It's wretched.*

KATY *bursts out laughing.*)

JENNIFER. You said you wouldn't laugh.

KATY. Who the hell put you in that?

JENNIFER. Shut up.

KATY. And what's with the holes in the stockings? Is that some kind of crack-ho chic?

JENNIFER. At least mine's a costume. Look at your outfit. You look like a little slut.

KATY. I'm not the one who's showing her tits to the world in a few minutes.

JENNIFER. Well half of Long Island has already seen yours.

KATY. But in a few minutes you're going to leapfrog right over me. You little slut.

JENNIFER. You're the slut.

(**KATY** *pokes* **JENNIFER.** **JENNIFER** *smacks her hand away.* **KATY** *struts in a circle around the couch as* **JENNIFER** *chases her. This goes on throughout this taunting.*)

KATY. Slut, slut, slut, slut, slut, slut, slut.

JENNIFER. At least I'm getting paid for what I'm doing.

KATY. Excuse me, whore.

JENNIFER. You're the whore.

KATY. Whore, whore, whore, whore...

JENNIFER. Hey there's an artistic side to this. I'm not just getting drunk and hooking up with some Hofstra frat boy.

KATY. Slut, slut, slut, slut, slut, slut, slut, slut...

JENNIFER. Stop it! Stop it!

(**JENNIFER** *screams. She stops chasing* **KATY** *and starts hyperventilating.*

KATY *realizes what she's done and runs over to her.*)

KATY. Oh my God. Don't do one of these. Calm down. Calm down.

(**KATY** *puts her arms around her and sits her on the couch, fanning her face.*)

JENNIFER. You're supposed to be here to make me less nervous and to make me feel more comfortable and less guilty.

KATY. I'm sorry. I'm just teasing you.

JENNIFER. Now I feel worse. I feel like a bigger slut than you.

KATY. Okay. I deserved that.

(**KATY** *holds her close.*)

JENNIFER. I don't want to do this anymore. This movie is going to suck and I'm showing my tits in it.

KATY. Why did you agree to it?

JENNIFER. Spencer, the director, is "it" right now. He's like the hottest underground talent out there. He has this cult following and everything. It seemed like a small price to pay at the time.

KATY. There's nothing small about your tits, baby.

JENNIFER. Oh God I know and they're going to be unleashed in a few minutes.

KATY. Hey look at the bright side. You're getting them on film before the move to Sag Harbor.

JENNIFER. That's not funny. You don't get this do you?

KATY. What am I supposed to get?

JENNIFER. Everyone in the world is going to see my breasts. Everyone. If I ever have kids, when they get to be teenagers, all their friends will be able to see this movie and say "I've seen your mom naked." And teenage boys all over America are going to be wearing out the pause buttons on their DVDs and well, you know. And my brother, my mother, my dad, my grandparents, they're all going to see me naked. And one day, when I'm dead, people will be able to put this movie on and see me naked. The world will own a piece of my naked body.

KATY. So quit.

JENNIFER. I can't. I signed a contract.

KATY. All contracts can be broken.

JENNIFER. My reputation would be shot. Like I said, Spencer's star is on the rise.

KATY. I don't understand that. I rented a couple of his

movies and I thought they sucked. They were like, laughably bad.

JENNIFER. They're very artsy.

KATY. Oh please. They're exploitation films.

JENNIFER. No offense but you probably didn't understand them.

KATY. Don't tell me. I have skinemax. I know exploitation when I see it. And it wasn't even good exploitation. But I have to admit that the shots of the clams and vaginas was awesome.

That was the funniest thing I've ever seen. But I have a hunch it wasn't supposed to be funny. Clams and vaginas. Yuck.

JENNIFER. Can you maybe find a way to say one thing that will make me feel better?

KATY. Sure. Just be glad you're not showing your clam in this movie.

(**JENNIFER** *starts crying.* **KATY** *puts her arm around her.*)

KATY (CONT'D) Everything is going to be fine.

JENNIFER. It won't be.

KATY. It will. It will be just like when we went to Mardi Gras and I pulled your top off in front of those hot guys. That wasn't a big deal was it?

JENNIFER. Are you kidding? I went to therapy for that. I still can't believe you did that. What is wrong with you? I don't understand –

KATY. Alright, alright. My point is that we should just have fun with it. Look, you have great boobs and you're going to show them off. And one day when we're old and we have to pick up our titties to tie our shoes, we'll look at this film and say, "look how hot you were."

JENNIFER. I hope you're right.

KATY. I am. I promise.

(**KATY** *pulls her in and hugs her.*)

JENNIFER. I love you.

KATY. I love you too.

(**SPENCER** *and* **KRISTOFF** *walk in.*)

SPENCER. Let's rock and roll! Let's rock and roll!

(*The girls stand to greet* **SPENCER**.)

JENNIFER. Spencer, this is my friend Katy.

SPENCER. It's a pleasure to meet you. And this grouchy bastard over here is our producer slash D.P. slash A.D. slash production manager Kristoff. Say hello, Kristoff.

(**KRISTOFF** *takes his place behind the camera and doesn't say hello.*)

SPENCER. So you're the one who's going to make this go smoothly for our mutual friend over here?

KATY. That's why I'm here. Oh and by the way I've seen all your films and I want you to know that I enjoyed them very much.

SPENCER. Jennifer, I love your friend. In all seriousness, thank you. I'm glad you enjoyed them. Jennifer, are we ready to get started?

JENNIFER. Yes.

SPENCER. Excellent. Let's do it.

KRISTOFF. Where the fuck is Barry?

SPENCER. Calm down. He's preparing.

KRISTOFF. He's had enough time prep time. Tell him to get his ass out here.

(**SPENCER** *kneels down next to* **KRISTOFF** *and talks to him. Neither of them notice as* **BARRY** *enters the stage. He is wearing just a towel.*)

BARRY. Let's do it!

SPENCER. See. Here he is. Barry we have a guest. This lovely young lady is Katy. Katy, this is Barry.

BARRY. Pleasure to meet you.

KATY. Oh my God. I've seen you on the soaps and I love you.

BARRY. Thank you.

KATY. You're even more attractive in person.

BARRY. Thank you. You're not so bad yourself.

SPENCER. I think I'm going to have you on every set I'm ever on. You're just a bundle of positive energy. Okay. Let's get started.

(**SPENCER** *gets up and turns around. He sees Barry's outfit.*)

SPENCER. Barry, what is that?

BARRY. I think the scene will be better if I'm wearing a towel.

KATY. He looks good in that towel.

KRISTOFF. Mother fucker! He's starting already. He's starting.

SPENCER. Just go put your pants on please. We have a very tight schedule.

KRISTOFF. He doesn't listen. He never listens!

(**KRISTOFF** *starts to move towards* **BARRY** *but* **SPENCER** *holds him back.* **BARRY** *just laughs.*

No one notices amid the chaos, but **JENNIFER** *starts breathing really heavy.*)

SPENCER. Barry, please go put your pants on.

BARRY. Alright, but it's your loss.

(**BARRY** *takes the towel off and tosses it at* **KRISTOFF**. *Barry is wearing just a sock over his package. This infuriates* **KRISTOFF** *further as he tries to chase after the bare-ass* **BARRY**.

BARRY *runs off the stage as* **SPENCER** *tries to hold* **KRISTOFF** *back.*

JENNIFER *looks like she's hyperventilating, but still no one notices.*)

SPENCER. Kristoff, you have to stay calm. You can't just fly off the handle like that.

KRISTOFF. But he starts with me. He's such an asshole. I don't know why you cast him. Barry, you're an asshole.

(**JENNIFER** *stands up and starts waving her hands around.*)

KATY. Oh my God. Jennifer!

(**JENNIFER** *nearly passes out but* **KATY** *gets to her in time and sits her on the couch.*)

KATY. Stop being nervous. You're going to be beautiful.

(**KATY** *starts slapping her slightly in the face.*)

JENNIFER. I'm okay.

(**KATY** *puts her arm around her, still smacking her.*)

KATY. You're going to be beautiful. Stop being nervous. You're beautiful.

(**KRISTOFF** *notices* **JENNIFER** *hyperventilating.*)

KRISTOFF. Oh great. Now what.

SPENCER. What's wrong with her?

KATY. She's nervous about being naked.

JENNIFER. Stop slapping me!

SPENCER. Let's get you up then.

(**SPENCER** *and* **KATY** *pick her up off the couch. They let her go. She nearly passes out again.* **KATY** *catches her and sits her back on the couch again.*)

SPENCER. Let's get her a drink.

JENNIFER. I just need to catch my breath.

SPENCER. Come on. We'll get you a drink. You'll feel better.

KATY. Just let her get some air.

(**KATY** *and* **SPENCER** *start waving their hands at her.*)

KRISTOFF. This is Barry's fault. He set everything off.

SPENCER. Kristoff, stop it.

KATY. How are you feeling, honey?

(**JENNIFER** *takes a deep breath. She coming out of it.*)

JENNIFER. Okay. I think I'm okay now. I'm sorry about

that.

KATY. Let's get you back to your stool.

(SPENCER *and* KATY *lead her back.*)

JENNIFER. I'm sorry, Spencer.

SPENCER. It's okay. It happens.

JENNIFER. Let's just do it.

KRISTOFF. We could just do it if Barry would get his ass out here.

SPENCER. Are you sure you don't want a drink?

JENNIFER. I'm positive.

SPENCER. You're positive?

KATY. She's positive. She's okay. She's tough. She's sexy. She can do this.

JENNIFER. Yeah. I just want to get this over with.

(KATY *cracks a smile, trying not to laugh.*)

JENNIFER. Are you laughing at me?

KATY. No. I'm thinking of something else. Just focus.

JENNIFER. You're lying. You're laughing at me.

(BARRY *comes back on stage wearing his jeans. He also has a few papers in his hands and a flex bar.*)

SPENCER. Barry, we have a nervous actress here. Let's get this done quickly for her.

BARRY. No problem.

SPENCER. Okay. Let's get going. Everyone is happy and we're all friends again, right? We weathered this ministorm, right? Let's bring a little levity to the situation here. We're making movies not curing cancer.

BARRY. He's right, you know.

SPENCER. Let's go.

BARRY. One second.

(BARRY *looks over his script.*)

KRISTOFF. Barry, why do you have a script? There are no lines in this scene.

BARRY. These are my own personal notes.

SPENCER. He can have notes. That's okay.

KRISTOFF. It's a sex scene. What does he need them for?

KATY. Most guys I've been with should have had notes.

SPENCER. Okay we have ourselves a little comedian over here.

(**BARRY** *puts down his notes.*)

BARRY. Okay. I'm ready.

KRISTOFF. Don't start with me, Barry.

SPENCER. We're ready to go. Let's go.

(**BARRY** *stands behind the couch.* **JENNIFER** *takes off her robe and sits on the stool.*

KATY *looks around*)

KATY. So this is what a real movie set is like?

SPENCER. No. This is what a Spencer Keyes movie set is like.

KRISTOFF. We have to get started.

KATY. Sorry.

SPENCER. No problem. There's nothing wrong with being curious and enthusiastic.

(**KRISTOFF** *gets the camera into position.*)

SPENCER (CONT'D) Now, Barry, I need you to slate the thing. It's right by your feet. Just hold it up and then when Kristoff gives you the go ahead, put it down.

(**BARRY** *picks it up.*)

BARRY. Like this.

(*He holds it up into position.*)

SPENCER. What can I say? The kid's a genius.

KATY. How come you don't have a guy to do that?

SPENCER. Well, one we're on a very, very tight budget. And two, it's a closed set and I didn't want anyone else around if it wasn't absolutely necessary.

KATY. Okay. Got it.

SPENCER. Great. Are we all ready?

KRISTOFF. Let's go.

SPENCER. Okay, let's do it. Camera.

KRISTOFF. Rolling.

KATY. Why is there no sound guy?

SPENCER. Cut.

KATY. I'm sorry.

SPENCER. It's okay. It's because this scene is being shot MOS.

KATY. MOS?

SPENCER. Without sound.

KATY. Without sound? How does MOS stand for without sound?

SPENCER. It's an old story. An old German director used to say,"We'll shoot this scene mit out sound."

KATY. Oh I see. It's a joke.

SPENCER. Kind of.

KATY. One more thing.

SPENCER. Sure.

KATY. Why would you shoot this without sound?

SPENCER. We're going to have music over it.

KATY. So we won't hear any moaning?

SPENCER. No.

KATY. That's good. I think hearing you moan, Jennifer, would make me very uncomfortable.

JENNIFER. Katy, I want to get this over with.

KATY. I'm sorry.

SPENCER. It's okay. She's curious. That's good. I like when people ask questions.

KRISTOFF. Alright. Let's roll.

SPENCER. Camera.

KRISTOFF. Rolling.

SPENCER. Slate it please, Barry.

(**BARRY** *holds the slate in front of the camera and puts* *it down.*)

SPENCER (CONT'D) Action.

> (**BARRY** *climbs over the couch, very catlike.* **JENNIFER** *sits on the stool, eyes closed, as if she's waiting for him.*
>
> *He comes up from behind her and kisses her neck.*
>
> *She lifts her head up into the air. He works his way down her neck.*
>
> **KATY** *laughs.*)

KRISTOFF. Cut.

JENNIFER. Katy!

KATY. I'm sorry. I thought it was mid out sound.

SPENCER. It is but the actors can hear you and that is distracting.

KATY. I understand. It won't happen again.

JENNIFER. Goddamit!

KATY. Alright. I said it won't happen again.

SPENCER. Okay let's go again. Camera.

KRISTOFF. Rolling.

SPENCER. Slate it, Barry.

> (**BARRY** *slates it.*)

SPENCER (CONT'D) Action.

> (**BARRY** *crawls over the couch and approaches her again.* **BARRY** *again kisses her neck. He starts to go down her neck. She lets out a pleasurable moan.*
>
> *Sensing the spot, he stays there. He kisses that spot again.*
>
> **JENNIFER** *laughs.*)

SPENCER (CONT'D) Cut.

BARRY. What's wrong? What did I do?

SPENCER. What happened?

JENNIFER. I'm sorry. I tried to hold it in.

> (**KATY** *starts laughing.*)

JENNIFER (CONT'D) Katy, stop laughing.

KATY. You laughed first.

JENNIFER. Because he hit my spot. Barry, that spot on my neck is very sensitive. It tickles.

BARRY. I'm sorry.

(KATY *keeps laughing.* JENNIFER *starts laughing too.*)

KRISTOFF. Can we all get the laugh out and move on please?

SPENCER. Kristoff, calm down. But let's do that. Let's all let the laugh out.

JENNIFER. I'm really sorry.

SPENCER. It's okay. Maybe that will loosen things up a little. Barry, avoid that spot.

BARRY. Will do.

JENNIFER. Okay. I feel better now.

KRISTOFF. Thank God.

SPENCER. Okay. Camera.

KRISTOFF. Rolling.

SPENCER. Barry.

(BARRY *slates it.*

They get started again. BARRY *crawls over the couch. He gets to her neck. He kisses it, but avoids the spot.*

He runs his fingers through her hair.

He kisses her on the lips. The kissing gets pretty hot. There's some heavy breathing. BARRY *starts for the neck again.*)

BARRY. You're rippin', baby. You're hot.

(BARRY *keeps going.* KATY *looks over at* SPENCER *and* KRISTOFF. *They are really into the scene.*)

BARRY (CONT'D) Your skin is so smooth, so supple. You're rippin'.

(JENNIFER *bursts out laughing.* KATY *follows.*)

SPENCER. Cut.

(JENNIFER *and* KATY *are still laughing.*)

JENNIFER. I'm sorry. I didn't expect that.

KATY. "You're rippin', baby?" What the hell is that?

BARRY. I was really getting into it. It just came out.

SPENCER. Is that absolutely necessary?

BARRY. It was getting pretty hot. I'm sorry. It just came out.

KATY. "You're ripping, baby." Rip, rip, rip...you are rippin!

KRISTOFF. Let's go.

SPENCER. Barry, just don't say anything. Let's leave it at that.

BARRY. Alright. Alright.

SPENCER. Now, Jennifer, this needs to look real. So it's gotta look hot. Remember, this is your fantasy. So, be uninhibited and enjoy it. Remember, you're not you. You're Candace and she's crazy about this guy. Go with that.

JENNIFER. I'm sorry, I was. I just didn't expect the whole rippin' thing.

SPENCER. I know but that's over now. So let's be pros here okay? So let's roll again. Camera.

KRISTOFF. Rolling.

SPENCER. Barry, just start in front of the couch. We have enough shots of you crawling over it by now.

(**BARRY** *slates it.*)

SPENCER (CONT'D) Action.

(*They go at it again.* **BARRY** *works his way down her neck.* **JENNIFER** *moans.* **BARRY** *works his way in front of her again. He kisses her. The kissing gets hot again.*

He grabs her chest. She jumps.)

JENNIFER. Ow.

KRISTOFF. I gotta' cut that.

SPENCER. Is everything okay?

JENNIFER. That was a little rough.

BARRY. No it wasn't.

SPENCER. Barry, come on.

BARRY. That wasn't rough.

JENNIFER. Do you have breasts?

BARRY. No.

JENNIFER. So how would you know if that was rough?

BARRY. I know my strength and I wasn't being rough.

JENNIFER. It felt rough.

SPENCER. Just be gentle. Please.

KATY. I have a question. Isn't this her fantasy? I don't think her fantasy would involve having her breasts manhandled.

SPENCER. This isn't her fantasy it's the character's.

KRISTOFF. Holy Christ. Let's just shoot the fucking scene.

KATY. So her character likes it rough?

SPENCER. She might.

KATY. She might? Didn't you write this?

JENNIFER. I'm ready to do this. Can he just not manhandle –

SPENCER. Well I like to leave a lot to the actor's imagination.

KATY. But not the audience?

SPENCER. What?

KATY. Why show her breasts at all? Why not leave that to the imagination of the audience?

JENNIFER. Katy, it's fine. Let's go.

SPENCER. When you have a fantasy, aren't you naked in it?

KATY. But you're missing the point. A fantasy –

KRISTOFF. Hey, whatever your name is. Can you just be quiet so we can move on?

KATY. I'm getting a little sick of your attitude. Go back behind your little camera and leave everyone alone.

KRISTOFF. Spence, I'm going to walk.

KATY. Good. Walk. You're probably a sucky camera guy anyway.

JENNIFER. I'm ready to do this.

SPENCER. Alright. Everyone stop. Barry, be more gentle.

Jennifer, just hang in there. Katy, just shut up. Kristoff, roll –

KATY. Just shut up?

SPENCER. Please be quiet.

KATY. You can say that but don't tell me to shut up.

SPENCER. I'm sorry.

KATY. That was rude.

SPENCER. I apologize. Can we move forward please?

KATY. I'm sorry too. Let's go.

SPENCER. Thank you. Barry, be gentle. Kristoff, roll.

KRISTOFF. Rolling.

(**BARRY** *slates it.*)

SPENCER. Action.

(*The start going at it again.* **BARRY** *works his hands down her back. He starts unzipping her corset. It starts to loosen.*)

JENNIFER. Wait.

SPENCER. Cut.

(**JENNIFER** *jumps up from the stool and fixes herself up.*)

JENNIFER. Okay. I'm ready to do this. I'm ready I swear it.

SPENCER. Then what's the problem?

JENNIFER. I need one thing first. If I could just get a quick shot of whisky or something. I'll loosen right up and that will be it.

SPENCER. I told you to have a couple of drinks before we started.

JENNIFER. I didn't want to do it then. It didn't feel right.

SPENCER. But now it does?

JENNIFER. I need it.

SPENCER. I'm afraid it's too late. Even if we had the time, I don't have anyone I can send to get you something.

JENNIFER. But I have –

KATY. Oh come on. You don't have an assistant on this set?

SPENCER. Do you see one? This is a low, no, it's a no budget film.

KATY. I can run and get something.

KRISTOFF. We don't have time to break.

JENNIFER. I have –

KATY. It will take ten minutes. We can find the time.

SPENCER. You don't know what you're talking about.

JENNIFER. Shut the fuck up, both of you! I am ready to do this. All I want is two shots of whisky. If you give me two shots of whisky I will whip my boobs out and you can shoot them and Barry can squeeze them and you can all watch and you can all get happy and I'll be naked in your stupid movie and you can all shut up and leave me alone but first I need some fucking whisky!

KATY. Calm down, honey. We'll get you some whisky.

SPENCER. We don't have time.

KATY. Yes we do!

SPENCER. No –

JENNIFER. I have some Jack Daniel's in my bag!

SPENCER. Oh. Okay. Where's your bag?

JENNIFER. In the holding room.

SPENCER. Hurry up and take your swig of whiskey. But when you get back we're doing this, right?

JENNIFER. Yes. I'll get naked just shut up.

BARRY. Bring me some whisky too.

KRISTOFF. No. You get nothing.

BARRY. Kristoff, why do you hate me so much?

SPENCER. Barry, just stop. Please. Jennifer, hurry.

(**JENNIFER** *runs off stage.* **SPENCER** *paces frantically.*)

KATY. I have a question. If you're such a hip hot director, how come you don't have any budget?

SPENCER. I self finance so I don't have to give up any creative control.

KATY. Do you think you have control issues?

SPENCER. I want things the way I want them.

KATY. Control issues.

SPENCER. I want my films to look the way I want them to look.

KATY. Control, control, control, control, control, control.

SPENCER. It's not control. It's –

KATY. Control, control, control, control, control –

KRISTOFF. Would you shut the fuck up?

KATY. Tell me to shut up again and I will bury that camera up your ass.

KRISTOFF. Come and get it.

> (**KATY** *starts towards* **KRISTOFF**. **SPENCER** *steps in her way.*)

SPENCER. Katy, please. We're almost done. Let's all try to be friends for five minutes.

> (**JENNIFER** *returns to the stage.* **KATY** *walks backwards and keeps her eyes on* **KRISTOFF**. *He taunts her. She points at the camera.*)

KATY. I'll break it.

KRISTOFF. I dare you.

> (**SPENCER** *pushes* **KRISTOFF** *back into position. He turns to* **JENNIFER**.)

SPENCER. Are we feeling better?

JENNIFER. I'm on an empty stomach so it will kick right in.

SPENCER. God I hope so.

KATY. I bet you do.

SPENCER. What is that supposed to mean?

KATY. Nothing. I'm sure this is all for artistic purposes.

SPENCER. I'm not going to get into this. Let's roll. Camera.

KRISTOFF. Rolling.

SPENCER. Slate the damn thing, Barry!

> (**BARRY** *slates it.*)

SPENCER (CONT'D) Action!

(*They start to go at it again.* **BARRY** *works his way down her chest. He grabs her chest again.*)

BARRY. Squeeze!

JENNIFER. Barry!

SPENCER. Cut.

JENNIFER. We just had a whole discussion about not doing that.

BARRY. That was gentle.

SPENCER. Don't touch her breasts again. Let's just shoot this thing.

KATY. I have one more question.

KRISTOFF. No.

KATY. I wasn't talking to you, Kristo.

KRISTOFF. It's Kristoff.

SPENCER. What is it? Come on.

KATY. Are you going to intercut this sex scene with shots of weird things pumping around and such to show some kind of obvious symbolism?

SPENCER. I don't do obvious symbolism.

KATY. What about the clams and vaginas?

SPENCER. I don't have time for this. Let's go.

KATY. No wonder you don't want any financial backing in your films, someone might make you take stupid scenes like that out of your movies.

SPENCER. You're the one who said you enjoyed my films.

KRISTOFF. Spence, let's go.

KATY. But I didn't say they were good.

SPENCER. You are a nuisance.

JENNIFER. My buzz is kicking in. Let's go.

KATY. You shouldn't have told me to shut up.

SPENCER. (*very effeminate*) Maybe that was good advice, honey.

KATY. Is that supposed to scare me?

JENNIFER. I have the buzz.

KRISTOFF. Spence, she's buzzing.

KATY. You don't scare me.

JENNIFER. Katy, shut up! I don't want to lose the buzz.

KATY. Fine. If she tells me to shut up. I'll shut up.

SPENCER. Thank God. Let's roll.

KATY. If you said it, you'd be out of luck.

KRISTOFF. Camera's rolling.

KATY. I don't even let my father tell me to shut up.

WHOLE CAST. SHUT UP!

(**KATY** *shuts up.*)

SPENCER. Forget the goddamn slate. Action.

(**JENNIFER** *starts laughing.*)

SPENCER. Cut!

(**JENNIFER** *keeps laughing.*)

SPENCER. We really must move forward. What is so funny?

JENNIFER. You.

SPENCER. Me?

JENNIFER. You have a secret.

SPENCER. I have a secret?

JENNIFER. "Maybe that was good advice, honey"

(*impersonating the effeminate tone.*)

Yeah. You can show all the tits and pussies in your movies that you want, but we all know your secret. And I'll leave it at that. And let's get naked.

(**KATY** *and* **BARRY** *are laughing.* **KRISTOFF** *is really pissed.*)

KRISTOFF. I'm shooting.

SPENCER. Yeah. Let's shoot this.

KATY. Why are you ignoring her? She made a legitimate point.

SPENCER. Camera.

KRISTOFF. Rolling.

SPENCER. Action!

JENNIFER. Wait. I have an idea.

SPENCER. Cut! What? What is it now?

JENNIFER. I'm totally ready and feeling the buzz but this request will make me more comfortable.

KRISTOFF. Holy shit!

SPENCER. I don't think there's anything that can make you more comfortable. You are nervous about showing your breasts and I can understand that.

KATY. No you can't.

SPENCER. Can I finish? But you're just going to have to deal with it.

JENNIFER. I promise. This will be it.

SPENCER. Fine. Can we get the scene done after this?

JENNIFER. Yes.

SPENCER. What's the request?

JENNIFER. I want everyone else to get into their underwear.

SPENCER. Excuse me.

(KATY *starts laughing.*)

JENNIFER. It would make me more comfortable.

SPENCER. That's ridiculous.

KRISTOFF. I'm out of here.

(KRISTOFF *storms off stage. No one seems to notice as they continue their argument.*)

KATY. I think it's fair.

JENNIFER. Julia Roberts made everyone do it on the set of one of her movies.

SPENCER. Honey, you are no Julia Roberts.

KATY. Hey, and you're no Martin Scorsese you third rate hack.

SPENCER. You be quiet!

KATY. You go shoot more clams and vaginas.

SPENCER. I can't believe this is happening.

KATY. Wait a minute. I just thought of something.

SPENCER. What now?

KATY. (*pointing at* **BARRY**) Are we going to see him naked?

SPENCER. No.

KATY. Why not?

SPENCER. Because we're not.

KATY. So we'll get nice close ups of her nipples but we won't get a glimpse of him?

SPENCER. We're seeing everything on him that we see on her.

(*The buzz is clearly kicking in now. As the others continue bickering,* **JENNIFER** *mumbles to herself, barely audible. No one pays attention to her.*)

BARRY. I show my ass in another scene.

(**SPENCER** *walks over to* **BARRY** *and* **JENNIFER.**)

SPENCER. She is showing her chest. And as you can see, Barry is showing his chest.

(**SPENCER** *puts his hand on* **BARRY**'s *chest.* **BARRY** *looks down at* **SPENCER**'s *hand.*)

BARRY. Please take your hand off of my chest.

SPENCER. Sorry.

BARRY. Why would you touch my chest? That's a little creepy.

SPENCER. I was just making a point.

KATY. A stupid point. You know a man's chest is not nudity. Now I want to see his penis in this movie.

BARRY. This is not the time or the place.

JENNIFER. No it's underwear time!

(**JENNIFER** *tugs at* **SPENCER**'s *pants. He shoves her off not really noticing what she's doing. She tries again. He ignores her. She undoes his belt and pulls on it.*)

KATY. Just go for it. Hey, Spence, it might even give your movie some credibility. Not a lot of films show penises.

SPENCER. I'm not showing his penis.

KATY. Sexist.

SPENCER. Goddmanit!

KATY. Don't get mad at me because I exposed you as a sexist.

(*He looks down and sees* **JENNIFER** *tugging at his pants. He throws her hands off and looks around. He notices* **KRISTOFF** *is gone. He heads off stage. But* **JENNIFER** *swipes his belt.*

She WHIPS it onto the stage like a lion tamer. She almost falls back in her drunken stupor.

KATY *moves closer to* **BARRY***.*)

KATY. Come on, Barry. You're a good looking guy. Show it.

BARRY. Don't hate the player, Katy, hate the game.

KATY. I don't even know what that means but I still think you should show your penis in this movie and...

(*She SCREAMS off stage.*)

KATY. Maybe Spencer can cut between your penis and hot dogs or something!

BARRY. Maybe Dutch hot house cucumbers!

JENNIFER. If everyone would just get down to their underwear, we can get this done.

BARRY. Nobody's here, sweetheart.

(**SPENCER** *and* **KRISTOFF** *return to the stage.* **KRISTOFF** *immediately takes off his pants and shirt, leaving him in his very tight, short black briefs.*)

KRISTOFF. There. Are you happy now?

SPENCER. Alright. If we all get in our underwear, will that shut you up? Can we get the scene done then?

JENNIFER. Yes. Hurry up.

(**SPENCER** *takes off his pants and he is wearing bikini-briefs, the same ones as* **KRISTOFF***.*

They each take a moment and notice that they are wearing matching underwear.

They step away from each other.

SPENCER *and* KRISTOFF *throw their clothes to the side.*

KATY *looks at them and laughs.*

They look back at her. She realizes they're looking at her.)

KATY. What are you looking at?

SPENCER. We're waiting.

KATY. I'm not doing it.

SPENCER. That was the deal.

JENNIFER. I don't care if she keeps her clothes on.

KRISTOFF. How is that fair to the rest of us?

KATY. You want to get your scene done? She's happy now. Get it done.

JENNIFER. Come on. I'm ready.

SPENCER. Okay. Let's just do it.

KRISTOFF. Oh no. We're all in this together now.

KATY. You can wait all day as far as I'm concerned.

JENNIFER. I don't want to wait any longer.

KRISTOFF. Then tell your friend to take off her clothes and we'll move on.

JENNIFER. Katy, just do it. It's just clothes. Who cares?

KATY. I'm not letting them see me in a thong.

SPENCER. Kristoff, come on. Let's do this. Let's get it over with.

KRISTOFF. Oh no. A minute ago she's screaming for Barry to show his penis but she can't get down to her underwear.

KATY. I'm not an actress.

KRISTOFF. That's right. Leave the set right now.

KATY. Fine.

(*She starts to walk away.* JENNIFER *grabs her.*)

JENNIFER. No. I need you here.

SPENCER. She can stay. Let's just shoot.

KRISTOFF. Then she has to be part of the team.

KATY. I'll make a deal with you.

(*She takes off her shirt. She looks damn good in that bra. She's busting out of it.*)

BARRY. Damn! You can choke an elephant with those.

KATY. I have.

SPENCER. Okay. Good enough.

KRISTOFF. No! After all that she's put us through she either gets with the program or she leaves. I'm tired of it, Spence. First I have to deal with Barry and his bullshit then we have to deal with Jennifer and her bullshit...

(*While **KRISTOFF** rants, **KATY** takes off her skirt behind his back.*)

KRISTOFF (CONT'D) And now this crazy bitch and she's not even in the movie.

KATY. Hey, Kristoff!

(*She throws her skirt right into **KRISTOFF**'s face.*

*He drops it onto the floor. He looks at her body. It's impressive. **SPENCER** can't help but look over too.*)

BARRY. You're slammin'.

KATY. Not rippin'?

BARRY. More than that, baby.

(***SPENCER** and **KRISTOFF** are still looking at her.*)

KATY (CONT'D) Stop staring.

(***KATY** shakes her ass as she seductively walks back to her position.*

She stands up against the wall.)

SPENCER. Let's go. Camera.

KRISTOFF. It's fucking rolling.

SPENCER. Action!

(***BARRY** kisses **JENNIFER**. He kisses her some more.*

*Something behind the couch catches **KATY**'s eye. She runs from her spot to grab it.*)

KRISTOFF. Cut! She ran into the frame.

SPENCER. What are you doing?

KATY. Just covering up.

(**KATY** *takes two pieces of paper from* **BARRY**'*s notes.*)

BARRY. Why are you taking my notes?

KRISTOFF. You don't need fucking notes!

(*to* **KATY**)

And you stay out of my frame!

(**KATY** *places one piece in the strap on one side of the thong and places the other piece on the other side. Now her ass is covered again.*

KATY *turns around and smacks her paper clad ass.*)

SPENCER. Just shoot.

KRISTOFF. Camera's rolling.

JENNIFER. Wait. I forgot something.

(**JENNIFER** *runs away.*)

JENNIFER. I'll be right back.

(*She runs off stage.* **KRISTOFF** *shakes his head.*)

BARRY. I can't work under these conditions, Spencer.

SPENCER. Shut the fuck up, you second rate soap bitch!

(**KATY** *laughs.*

SPENCER *starts throwing a complete and total tantrum. He starts swinging and pounding away at the couch, punching the hell out of it.*)

SPENCER. Fuck, fuck, fuck, fuck, fuck, fuck, fuck, fuck, fuck....
Fuck, fuck, fuck, fuck, fuck, fuck, fuck, fuck, fuck...

(**KATY** *and* **BARRY** *look on in amusement.*

BARRY *mimics the punching.* **KATY** *laughs.*

KRISTOFF *checks his watch. Enough is enough.*

KRISTOFF, *of course still in his underwear, takes his water bottle over to Spencer and taps him on the shoulder.*

SPENCER *stops the tantrum and turns around.* KRIST-OFF *throws the water in his face.*

SPENCER *calms down immediately.*

KRISTOFF *proceeds to rub the water out of* SPENCER*'s eyes.*

One guy in his underwear rubbing the eyes of another guy in his underwear.)

KRISTOFF. There. Are you okay?

KATY. Wow. That's so gay.

KRISTOFF. He's not gay, he's just an asshole.

(JENNIFER *returns to the stage. She keeps grabbing her breasts and adusting them.* SPENCER *shakes the cobwebs out of his head.*)

JENNIFER. Let's do this.

(*She keeps fussing with her chest. She won't leave them alone.*)

SPENCER. Jennifer, we're about to shoot so would you please stop playing with your breasts?

BARRY. That's my job.

SPENCER. Alright. Camera.

KRISTOFF. Rolling.

BARRY. Wait. I need to take a look at my notes.

KATY. Come and get 'em.

(BARRY *starts away from the couch.* KATY *turns her ass around towards* BARRY. *She smacks her ass to taunt him.* SPENCER *cuts* BARRY *off and pushes him back towards the couch.*)

SPENCER. Get back!

KRISTOFF. We're shooting! Camera's rolling!

(BARRY *starts in on* JENNIFER. *They're getting really into it.*

He undoes the top button. Then the next one. Then the next one.

We see the middle of her chest.

He grabs each side of the corset.

Everyone looks on in anticipation.

He pulls it open and...

JENNIFER *is wearing a strapless bra under the corset.*

KATY *laughs.*)

SPENCER. This is the stupidest day of my life.

    (**KATY** *continues to laugh.*)

    Jennifer, why in the name of God are you wearing two bras?

JENNIFER. I'm sorry. I can't do it. I just can't. I thought I could. But I don't want to show my boobs. I'm not ready.

    (**SPENCER** *paces and talks to himself. He's losing it.*)

BARRY. Spence, this might work. I can tear that off.

KRISTOFF. Let him tear it off!

JENNIFER. You're not tearing my bra off.

BARRY. It won't hurt. We can get you some cream from the makeup girl.

JENNIFER. What are you talking about?

BARRY. Some boobie cream so it won't hurt.

KRISTOFF. Get her the boobie cream and tear it off!

SPENCER. There's no such thing. Everyone shut up!

BARRY. Trust me. It will be hot. I'll slide the corset off and then tear this baby off. Now that's a fantasy.

SPENCER. Barry, you are the dumbest fuck I have ever met. Please don't say another word and just stand there and look pretty. Now Jennifer, this is a problem.

JENNIFER. I know. But there's nothing I can do. I can't do it.

SPENCER. Holy shit! It's tits. It's a goddamn pair of tits. What's the big deal? It's a small independent film. Who's going to know?

JENNIFER. So if it's just a small independent film that no one's going to know about? Why should I bother to show my breasts?

KATY. Yeah.

SPENCER. You shut up!

KATY. I told you not to say that to me.

KRISTOFF. I told you not to let her bring a friend, Spence. I told you.

BARRY. I really think I should just tear it off.

JENNIFER. Barry, you are sick. You are a sick fuck.

BARRY. I'm not the one wearing two bras.

JENNIFER. What? Take two steps back from me right now.

SPENCER. Everyone, shut the fuck up! I'm calling the shots. This is my set, this is my film!

KATY. Your movies suck big dick.

SPENCER. Well you and me have something in common then.

KATY. Really? Whose dick are you sucking? Kristo's?

SPENCER. No I meant that –

KATY. Of course not. He doesn't have a big dick. He's got a little winky one...

(*She jerks off one of her fingers, pretending it's Kristoff's small penis.*

KRISTOFF *charges away from the camera and gets right in* **KATY**'s *face.*)

KRISTOFF. I have never in my life hit a woman

KATY. They'd probably all kick your ass anyway.

KRISTOFF. But right now I'm –

(*BOOM!* **KATY** *knees him in the balls.* **KRISTOFF** *hits the ground.*

SPENCER *runs over to him.* **KATY** *runs to the other side of the stage. She hides behind* **JENNIFER**.)

SPENCER. What did you do that for?

JENNIFER. He was threatening her.

SPENCER. He wasn't going to do anything. He's a pacifist.

JENNIFER. He was still threatening her.

KATY. Yeah. I don't take that. I don't like being threatened and I don't like being told to shut up.

BARRY. Katy, can I take a look at my notes?

KATY. Be my guest.

(*She turns around to show him her ass again but* **JEN-NIFER** *steps in front of them.*)

JENNIFER. No. Barry can wait. And put this on.

(*She grabs her robe and gives it to* **KATY**.

KRISTOFF *is writhing around on the floor.*)

SPENCER. Jennifer, are you going to do this or not?

JENNIFER. No. I can't.

SPENCER. You are without a doubt the most unprofessional actress I've ever worked with. You will go nowhere in this business I promise you that.

KATY. Like you're an authority on that.

SPENCER. I'm pretty well connected. People know me.

KATY. People know you suck.

SPENCER. This is a breach of contract by you. I can sue you.

KATY. She doesn't have anything.

SPENCER. I can still make things miserable for her.

JENNIFER. I have an idea.

KATY. You don't scare us.

SPENCER. Her name is mud from now on.

JENNIFER. I said I have an idea.

KATY. Her name is mud? Is that a line from one of your shitty movies?

SPENCER. Make fun of me all you want –

KATY. I will.

JENNIFER. Shut the fuck up both of you. I have an idea.

SPENCER. No more ideas.

KRISTOFF. (*struggling*) No more ideas.

(*to* **KATY**)

Fuck you.

JENNIFER. You're going to like this one.

BARRY. I want to hear it.

KATY. Me too.

SPENCER. No. You're finished.

JENNIFER. Okay. What if Katy gets in the scene too?

KATY. What?

SPENCER. What?

BARRY. Keep going.

JENNIFER. It can be like a lesbian threesome scene.

KATY. There is no way I would ever appear in one of his movies.

JENNIFER. Just hear me out.

SPENCER. Who is getting naked?

JENNIFER. Nobody.

SPENCER. No. No deal.

JENNIFER. Let me finish. Barry and I will do the everything we just did, but when we get to the part where he's supposed to take my top off, we can cut to the bed where Katy is in bed with us.

KATY. I'm not doing it.

JENNIFER. It will be fun.

SPENCER. Do I get a kiss out of this?

JENNIFER. We'll each kiss Barry.

SPENCER. No, no, no. Either one of you gets naked, or both of you get naked or you make out with each other in the scene.

BARRY. I think the idea works. But I still think I should rip off some piece of clothing. Katy, can I rip that bra off?

KATY. Not on film.

BARRY. That's promising.

SPENCER. I'm afraid it doesn't make sense.

KATY. None of your movies make sense.

JENNIFER. It's a fantasy sequence. We never have to even know who she is.

SPENCER. Alright, if you make the make out thing look hot, I'll go for it.

BARRY. I'll go for it.

JENNIFER. It's all up to you, Katy.

KATY. What will I wear?

SPENCER. Wear that.

KATY. No.

SPENCER. We'll get you into wardrobe and get you something.

KATY. Can I kiss Barry's chest?

BARRY. Yes.

KATY. And I want to see his penis.

(**SPENCER** *shakes his head.* **BARRY** *leans in and whispers something to* **KATY**.)

KATY. I'll do it.

SPENCER. Alright. Everyone take a break. Katy, let's get you into wardrobe and Kristoff, let's get you some ice. Pretty boy, come with me.

BARRY. Wait, Spence.

(**BARRY** *calls* **SPENCER** *over and points at the girls.*)

BARRY. Is there going to be enough room on camera for all four of those breasts?

(**SPENCER** *shoves* **BARRY** *off stage.* **BARRY** *smirks as* **SPENCER** *follows him out.* **KRISTOFF** *gets off the ground gingerly and follows them.*)

KRISTOFF. We need to re-light.

(**JENNIFER** *drops herself down to the couch.* **KATY** *sits right next to her.*)

KATY. Thanks for inviting me. That was interesting.

JENNIFER. It looks like it's going to get even more interesting.

(**BARRY** *comes back onto the stage.*)

BARRY. Katy, I need my notes.

KATY. Take them.

(*She stands up and sticks her ass out at him. He RIPS those pieces of paper out of there.*

BARRY. Thanks.

(*He SMACKS her on the ass. She YELPS.*

BARRY *throws the notes to the ground and leaves the stage.*)

KATY. He's nasty. I like it.

JENNIFER. No, no. You don't want any of that.

KATY. What do you mean?

JENNIFER. He hooked up with the make up girl and she said he gave her crabs.

KATY. Come on! That sucks.

(**SPENCER,** *still in his underwear, runs back out onto the stage.*)

SPENCER. Let's go!

(*He runs off stage. The girls laugh.* **JENNIFER** *gets up and starts to leave.* **KATY** *grabs her arm, stopping her.*)

KATY. Two to one I can get Spencer to show me his dick.

JENNIFER. Deal.

(*They leave the stage. The lights go down.*)

Also by
Matt Morillo...

ALL ABOARD
THE MARRIAGE HEARSE